# THE COYOTE CRIED TWICE

**ALSO BY AUSTIN BAY**

A Quick and Dirty Guide to War
(with James F. Dunnigan)

# THE
# COYOTE
# CRIED
# TWICE

## AUSTIN BAY

ARBOR HOUSE / NEW YORK

*Designed by Richard Oriolo*

Manufactured in the United States of America
10 9 8 7 6 5 4 3 2 1

Library of Congress Cataloging in Publication Data
Bay, Austin.
The coyote cried twice.
I. Title.
PS3552.A8586C6   1985      813'.54      85-7519
ISBN: 0-87795-728-2 (alk. paper)

For Monroe Spears,
Lois Powell, and
Mary Louise Yoe

# 1

THREE MEXICANS DROVE INTO the roadside park just east of Benavides and I rolled off the concrete picnic table, trying to shake the early morning chill from my knees and elbows.

But calling them Mexican is inaccurate. All three men were pure Tex-Mex, as in howdy and buenos dias, the real bi-cultural breed with straight black shocks of Indian hair and pearl button shirts. I sized them up and figured I stood a fifty-fifty chance with the friendliest face, so I asked the smiley dude if I could catch a ride and he replied with a put-on Texas drawl, as in y'all climb y'all self in the back, y'heah? Hey, there's no all in this act, I told him, there's just one of me and he said good, that'd be one less to watch. Then this other dude, the smooth one, the honcho in control, asked me where I was going. I shrugged. Did it make any difference?

The boss hoss finished taking a piss—that was why they'd stopped in the first place—then he gave me a cool sort of look. I didn't know how to take the guy 'cause he had a pair of educated eyes, something I didn't expect from a Tex-Mex cowboy in a half-ton pickup truck. "Then where're you coming from?" he asked, a faint trace of Latino in his voice. "Or doesn't that make any difference?" Hey, I thought, good comment. The guy had snap and moved like a natural—with positive cool, control, and a back about six times as dry as mine.

"Uh, Michigan, De-troit area," I said, sitting down on a big toolbox bolted to the pickup's rear bed. "I was raised up in Oklahoma, but that's a long time back."

"De-troit, huh?" He gave a grunt. "I understand that's a pretty rough proposition. You bailing out of Yankee land?" He picked up an empty beer car from the asphalt and tossed it into the back of the truck. It hit near my feet. "Did the assembly line shut down?"

"Yeah," I replied, but my yeah was halfway toward a lie. Giving these dudes a laundry list of odd jobs, layoffs, and CETA projects would be a waste of time, though time was about the only thing I had to waste.

"My name's Paco," the head honcho said, reaching over the truck side to shake my hand. "Paco Ramirez. That's Joe back in the brush taking a crap." I nodded. Yeah, Joe was taking a crap. "Big Tex there is Fernando when it isn't Fred." Paco nodded toward the man with the smile and the fakey drawl. I shook Paco's hand. He had a vise for a grip.

"I'm Bill Buchanan."

"I hope you can handle the sixty-mile-an-hour ventilation, amgio."

"I like flying low."

Paco gave me another cool sort of look, then rapped the pickup with his palm. "C'mon people. Let's get finito and roll."

Fernando muttered something about working all night.

A couple of minutes later Joe stepped out of the mesquite thicket and the three of them climbed back in the cab.

As the pickup accelerated, I squeezed between two rolls of canvas tarp and put my head against my pack. This would be a good chance to catch some snooze, I thought, though I didn't really need any more sleep. I'd had lots of chances to sleep. On my first ride the night before—a moving van caught just south of Sugar Land—I'd nodded off to some classical sounds piped out of a pair of rubber headphones. The van man, who said he came from Chicago, also had a stack of Dixieland tapes, jivey tunes I checked out between dreams, and we got along real well, him driving, me nodding between the phones, until around two in the morning, when he called it a very long day and pulled off into a truck stop just west of Robstown. In the diner I got a shot of coffee and was asking another trucker about a lift when this weirdass dude with a clerical collar sidled up to the counter and asked me if I wanted a ride in his, quote, "hot little Vette." He said he was a Baptist minister going to a lay preachers' convention in Nuevo Laredo. I should have figured something was about wrong. But I didn't figure. Laredo sounded farther west, so I said yeah. What a mistake. He drove like a mad bat out of a blast furnace, with his radar Fuzzbuster for sonic eyeballs; then toward three o'clock in time, near wherever his flight speed had brought us, he checked his watch and tuned the car radio to some million-watt Mexican station that spoke God's Own English. With the Sound of Glory Sisters humming in the hymnal background we listened to Country Clyde the Cowboy Preacher spew forth about Blackening Sin, Forty-Dollar Prayer Shawls, 'Bandoned Lambs, Blessed Lottery Tickets, Acceptable Edens, and the True Blood. "Amen amen," Clerical Collar repeated, his amens sounding like Country Clyde's without static. " 'Bominations of the

Dust," screamed Country Clyde, "the Dirt, the falling fall-ing Earth," radio static, "blood failures." Oh Christ. Then the Glory Sisters hummed. "Amen," said Clerical Collar once more, as he turned the car's heater to a BTU level that would bubble anybody's hemoglobin.

So I asked him what the deal was, man. The summer night might get a little chilly but we weren't in Antarctica.

"Well, boy," the Collar said, "if you're *that* hot, I guess you could pull off your pants. But don't struggle with the belt. Poor bodies just get themselves wrecked by leather belts."

Shit, I thought, I'm stuck in a Corvette with a born-again queer. "Hit the brakes, padre," I told him.

But pain, he began, pain, everyone in hopeless pain, but no pain like his, no awful shackles like his, his amens, his lonely brain, the leather, and the lead foot on the accelera-tor. No way out, he said.

"Crapola."

I grabbed the wheel. The Vette ripped sideways as he hit the brakes. He cursed. The car straightened and stopped. He cursed again.

"You can goddamn well walk, good buddy," Collar said.

"Yeah." I reached for the lock.

Then a ragged grin ran across his face, a couple of teeth sticking into his lower lip. "But this is the middle of no-where," he said with a candy-laced drawl, "you've no idea where you are."

Opening the door so that the dome light would shine, I grabbed a Texas road map from the dash and popped it against my chest. "No idea, huh? In five minutes I'll get me an idea. And you give ole Baptizing Clyde—iffn you ever see him—a wink from me, y'heah?"

The preach's neck above his white collar turned a red sort of purple and he began to say that he'd been grie-vously misunderstood. Or something. I slung my pack over my shoulders and slammed the front door. He jammed the Vette in gear and took off with a tire-biting rain of gravel and dust.

 Mid-nowhere. Dead right. So I'd gone and gotten myself shoveled again. The Vette's lights faded into a blunt road of nothing lined by mesquite. What a bitch. Take a step, any step, and start a hike. The legs found a pace and heels hit gravel until mid-nowhere turned into a roadside park—pre-cast concrete tables surrounded by four thousand vacant cans and loose heads of rotting lettuce. I washed my face in a water fountain's cold rush, then pulled my survival blanket out of my pack and went to sleep atop the one clean and bugless picnic table, keeping the old buck knife open in my palm. The preach wouldn't be coming back, but you can never be too cautious, or too asleep, when you crash in a roadside park. For some folks the idea of money is worth more than a life, and in hard times you can't even trust the cops not to try and take your change.

 So the sound of a truck, Paco's truck, had awakened me. Yeah, these guys seemed all right, genuine farm boys, a good ride to somewhere.

 Pulling the road map out of my coat pocket, I got down closer to the truck bed and tried to avoid the wind. Yeah, there was Benavides, and we seemed to be on the road toward, what, Chorillo, a dot in Duval County. Where the hell was that? I gave the map a flip and found I was south of San Antone. Man, had I done me some traveling since I left Saint Louis, super-traveling since I left Portland.

 And had I ever screwed up in Oregon. Flopped in the woods, belly-landed among those endless woods.

 I should never have told those guys at the lumber company I'd flown a chopper in Nam.

 Naw, why go and fault myself, why keep your mouth shut when you're proud? I'd been a Snake pilot, as in

Cobra and rat-ta-tat-tat—even made warrant officer 2—
and me and a couple of guys got to talking about Nam, like
everybody does whether they were there or not, and I said
yeah, I'd flown both fixed wing and rotorbirds. It was the
stone-sober truth—no lies, no tarnish. And then the mill
brass got word of it. Can yah still fly? the manager asked,
sort of sly like, but I didn't pay any attention to the sly-
ness. I told the execs I hadn't been fixed for a civilian license and all the other bureaucratic red tape, and I hadn't
had a second of rated time in eleven or twelve years. I
didn't try to put much over. But Waldonworld Incor-
porated of Bend, Oregon, didn't care about all that. They
didn't care about a lot of things, silly things like laws and
paperwork and basic helicopter mechanics. A blind man
could see that Waldonworld Papermill's copter mainte-
nance set a new record for dismal, and Ace Buchanan
isn't blind. I've got a pair of calibrated eyeballs, when I've
got a notion to see through them. Still Waldonworld's sly-
talking management saw a chance to get a semi-cheap
pilot, while trying vigorously—they had to promise me
they were trying—to get me some papers.

I took one look at their bright red Jet Ranger and said I
could fly anything manufactured by Bell. Man, had I
logged some times in Hueys, I told them. They said they
were processing the paperwork, then they flashed the
bonus cash. Money—we had us a going deal.

So the first week I made the regular runs out to the log-
ging sites, and the bird works perfectly and everything's
tight. Then the screw job comes. Hey, Buchanan, big mission and the other pilot's sick, shouldn't be any problem
from your angle, should there, why you'll get to fly out of
the woods.

But I like the woods, I said. Tough luck, they said.

So we had to be flying into this little airfield near Corvallis, taking some Waldonworld lumber executive up

there to give a speech at Oregon State, when the tail rotor flies off and I manage to land the bucking bitch. And who should be there, down on the field, but some just-in-the-neighborhood FAA inspector. Christ, the only thing worse would have been some 51-caliber Vietcong.

Man, you're some hoss, old friendly FAA says, you're a real hot-seat pilot. He's hyper-impressed with my ability and it's all smiles and groove talk and pats on the back until he starts what you might call a pre-preliminary courtesy good-ole-boy inspection and he finds out—after a look at the wreck, at a fudged logbook, and after a couple of sharpening phone calls and you-better-stick-arounds—that yours truly's completely undocumented—by damn, not even applied for—and that's like telling a bureaucrat I'm the anti-Christ.

And it's all my fault, right? The lumber exec just smiles and shrugs and heads for Oregon State, and I'm left there by the crash.

Well, maybe Waldonworld Papermill did know where to put some political money or something, 'cause after about twenty-four hours of sweating in a Corvallis motel I get a phone call that says I won't get investigated and do jail time—get that, I won't do jail time—if I'll just disappear, okay, slide off to unpaid freedom, as in one asshole and two elbows pounding 'way into the distance?

I knew I was being had. It wasn't the first time. Yup, the powerful had stuffed this Bill before, in the face and butt.

So I knew what to do. I said yes sir, you bet, thanks for the advice, and yes I'll keep my mouth shut. Shut tight. You can't fight the big boys on their own turf—their turf being the courts and the jails and the banks. Just say yas-suh and let your anger slide. Why break your head? If you grow old and fat and happy, then it won't matter any more. But—and this is the big but, I've learned that, too—if you can't digest anger, if it stays nasty and aches in your craw, then your only hope's the jungle, that zone away, the turf where you can wait, and think, and plan, then wait some more. Maybe you wait forever, and maybe you don't, but you're out of their terrain, into a space where your anger has a chance.

Lord, yeah. I thought about all that as I hung up the phone, then hung down my head.

So I caught a bus back to Bend and went through my two bags of clothes and my pack. The company had me living in a mobile home with a couple of Canadians and a Polish exile. The foreigners chipped in and bought my bags for ten bucks apiece. Out at the lumber lot the straw boss handed me an envelope with a thousand bucks in cash. "I'm telling you to just get good and lost, huh, Buchanan?" he said, staring at the ground. "There's a shitfire going on about that chopper." He raised a queasy kind of eye. I looked at the cash careful like and said, yeah, okay, there probably was a fire—I tried to catch his eye again—but I sure figured I had, maybe, some more coming to me?

He didn't move. Not just yet. "You short already?" he said. "Payday was just last week and I knowed you took yours in cash."

Yeah, I said. Maybe I should get paid by mail, but there was this long weekend down in Winnemucca. I checked his queasy eye. Seems, I continued, seems the northern Nevadan desert economy had sort of soaked my eight hundred bucks into its dusty gut. All I remembered were lots of bottles and a redhead snuggling next to me while I watched a Bogart flick on the motel's cable channel. I jabbed my finger in the straw boss's chest. Could he identify with that?

I jabbed him again. He swallowed.

Maybe, maybe he could identify with, I put a finger on his neck, with something like that?

He stood there, then sort of twitched his neck away

from my hand. "Heck, you ain't a bad sort of guy, Buchanan," he said, this time trying to look me straight in the eye. "You should have stayed around and been a logger instead of shooting your mouth off and getting fancy with that chopper business."

Well yeah, I agreed, but wasn't that an easy thing to say since the past had already done its thing? Huh? And, friend, we're dealing with now. A very level right now.

I still hadn't clenched my fist.

He reached into his wallet and took out another four hundred bucks. His hands shook, just a twinge. "You don't have this comin' to you, but, fella, the job market's gone straight to hell. I got some sympathy with that, you know, and well, you ain't been fairly dealt so . . . so take it." He gave me the second pile of cash.

I looked at him hard. He turned an alcoholic sort of red. "Hey, Bill, uh, you don't think I was trying to hold out on you the first time, huh?" He flustered. "That's your money. I want you to have it . . . you gotta have it."

"Right," I said. I had figured this game. "Gee, I'm glad you could find this extra dough. Paycheck from a ghost, huh?"

"Hey, I'm clean with you, Buchanan."

Clean through. But I felt a little better. They were giving a lot of bucks to somebody who'd trashed a chopper. Okay, maybe they were afraid of me. "You know," I said, tapping the straw boss on his turning shoulder, "you're just like the whole fucking company—sleazy and disgusting."

He was on his last ounce of guts, but like somebody who'd been through it before, he knew if I decked him he could crawl off and get back up. "Christ, fella, wise up and hit the road. We don't want any hassles with the government or with some crazy smartass." He walked off like he wanted to run.

I grinned and split, for Portland, then Helena, then Rapid City, then Detroit.

Detroit. Oh, was that ever stupid, as well as sleazy and disgusting. The economy was on its downslide roll and a nonunion dude like me didn't have a chance. I went to Lansing and tried to check out my old welding job. No dice. The old boss was still ragged. The girl was still mad. So I went down to Saint Louis and that was another mistake. Nobody had anything for anybody in Saint Louis, except an unemployment check, and only the lucky were getting those. I got down to about seven hundred bucks and I'd been watching my resources pretty closely—no blondes, no redheads, no motels with cablevision. Man, I watched my dollars and always counted the change. But money can only buy so much time and the thought of two three-dollar dinners a day and an eight-dollar room for the next fifty nights just didn't turn me on. Didn't that make seven hundred bucks? And that budget didn't include dimes for the pay toilet. Plan it out, babe. I made up a hundred-day budget and then puked. No Salvation Army for me.

Then I tried to call my Great Aunt Doe down in Ponca City, and after a couple of days of ringing a neighbor answered the phone. Aunt Doe had gone back to the old folks home and I could reach her there. I jotted down the number, then crammed it in my pocket. Other than Cousin Pete in Albuquerque, Doe was my last living relative. The poor old thing loved me, but I couldn't take her social security pennies. Naw, I wouldn't call her until I got me a job someplace, then I'd go see her and give her a present, if she weren't dead by then.

I called Cousin Pete's place and talked with his wife, Alberta. Would Pete mind if I came out for a week and looked for work? Nope, she said, not as long as I shared the expenses, but I'd better not arrive thinking I was going to find some instant gold mine. The West was starting to fill up with unemployed exiles from back East. "This ain't no frontier," she said.

When I told her I'd gotten unemployed in Oregon, she just snickered.

So I caught a truck from Saint Louis to Fort Smith, then got one long ride to Houston via Texarkana. Man, in a gnat's ass I'd had enough of Houston. It was one gridlocked traffic jam on a freeway that was no way, and the old man who'd picked me up in Fort Smith was already about three breaths from being an emphysema statistic. Houston's pollution just choked him by his dying throat. He coughed incessantly and kept telling me about how he wished he'd never started smoking and it was such goddam hell to try and quit at sixty-four. "Seems like nothing can be done," he said.

And I started coughing, too, from the humidity and the auto fumes that mixed into an oppressive urban soup. I cursed it all, then knew better. That's the smell of the road, and if you can't afford to go by air, you'd better get used to the grit.

# 2

I WOKE UP WHEN the pickup stopped. A couple of stray dogs, dogs that were ragged bundles of scabs and fur, barked spit in my face as I crawled out the tailgate and looked around.

There simply wasn't much to Chorillo, Texas. La Fiesta Cafe's neon sign flashed its hot pink message in the morning light. Across a stretch of gravel parking lot stood one of the earth's most decrepit gas stations. Source Oil Company-Gasoline Marketing Division, a space heavy on grease, dirt, and bureaucratese. Next to the gas station stood a smoky-looking house made of concrete blocks with a painted scrawl on its side reading BAR-B-Q right over a more official looking sign that said POST OFFICE—IN-SIDE. On the far side of this semi–post office, farther down the road, stood another building and behind it a wood frame shack.

"Welcome to Chorillo," Paco said.

"This all there is to it?" I asked with a yawn.

"There's couple of houses over in those oaks, and a store down the road." I looked across the highway. In a clump of pin oaks I saw a mobile home and a cluster of wooden shacks. About two hundred yards farther down the highway, separated from the asphalt road by a wide swath of gravel, stood a long white building I took to be the store.

"You int'rested in eating?" Fernando said. He was asking.

We went into the La Fiesta and inside I laid eyes on one of the nicest pairs of calves I'd seen since Winnemucca. Yeah. Her black hair fell like dark rain over the white blouse. The apron bow around her waist, instead of domesticating her slim figure, made it even more sensual. My eyes must have stared like two fried eggs, both sunny side up.

"Cram it up your ass," she told me after I let loose a long, low whistle.

"You like Doreta?" Joe asked. I nodded. "Well, don't like her too much."

"How come," I said, looking over the menu and trying to decide between scrambled eggs and French toast.

"Because she's Fernando's," Joe replied in a loud voice, "and Fernando carries one big knife." Fernando laughed, then told Joe to shut up before his face became part of the table.

"I am not Fernando's," Doreta said.

"Not yet, Chiquita," Fernando winked, "but it's only a matter of time."

Joe and Fernando ordered scrambled eggs and Paco went for fried. I had the French toast.

"So what do you boys do besides hustle waitresses?" I asked, trying to sound macho. I figured this was their turf and all, and a little of the Latin tough guy vocals might do me some good.

Joe scratched his unshaved face and looked at Paco. "Hey, Pock, what do we do?"

Paco shrugged. "Right now some of us are running fence."

"Right now some of us are running fence," Joe repeated.

Fernando said he sometimes drove a truck in San Antonio "and sometimes I answer phones." He looked at Paco. "Want to trade some postholes for a desk?"

"The ranch business is shit," Paco said quietly. "And you young guys talk too much."

"You a rancher?" I asked. Paco nodded a lazy yes. I smiled. "Wow, I didn't think they let a Mex own property in Texas."

The line didn't fly at all. "Guess you're just ignorant, *bolio,*" Paco replied smoothly, "and sort of stupid." He let the silence sink in a moment. "Actually right now I'm a foreman." I turned red and took a bite of stale French toast. Then Joe started talking about how the Astros had suddenly gotten hot and that Jose Cruz was Jesus Christ with a bat, and I decided to keep my mouth shut as long as I was in South Texas. A guy like me didn't have much to say anyway. As it was, I'd almost said spic instead of Mex and saying spic in Chorillo would be like saying nigger in Harlem, wop in Rome or kike in Jerusalem—you know, popping off the kind of racist jive that gets you killed by other racists. Like Paco said I was stupid, a *bolio,* Tex-Mex Spanish for dumbshit white boy in redneck rags. Next time I'd git hip and go with Chicano—see, sometimes even I can figure out how to score.

If I got a next time. Guess these dudes had it in for me.

But they let it all ride so I let it ride and we ate and talked baseball. Joe and Fernando got in an argument about Valenzuela's screwball, then Paco got up from the table to get something out of his windbreaker. He'd brought the jacket in draped across his arm; otherwise, I would have seen the Black Horse patch sewn squarely on the right front pocket. Well, I'm noticing now, I thought.

"You in the Eleventh Cav, Paco?" I asked.

"Yeah."

"Same here."

"Hmm," he said, pulling a twenty-dollar bill out of the jacket. I couldn't tell if what I'd said meant shit to him or if he was still half-pissed or whether he was just distracted, thinking about something else. "Nam?" he asked as he sat down.

"Yeah. Air Cav Troop."

"That was a crazy bunch of guys," he said, taking a sip of coffee. "You there for the Michelin?"

"I wasn't allowed to miss it."

He nodded. "I made that fight in Fox Troop. I'll hate rubber trees the rest of my life."

"I can understand that."

"Bad place to stage a slaughter. We shouldn't have gone in there."

"That's a fact, amigo," I said, scratching my unshaven chin. "We got used and a-bused."

Paco sort of looked at me—then drained the cup.

"Anybody want any more coffee?" Joe asked. No one did so Joe yelled for Doreta. "Do I get a kiss with the check?" he called.

He didn't get a kiss but he got the bill—and Paco picked up my tab. I started to say no. "Hey, man, forget it," Paco said. "If you were laid off in De-troit, I'm sure you can use a little welfare." I looked the guy straight in the pupils and said thanks from the bottom of my gut. I guess I still had close to six hundred bucks, but after that ran out, well, it looked as if the world could get pretty cold even in the hundred-degree heat of a Texas high noon.

"That's real decent of you."

"Paco's a big-time spender," Fernando winked. "Besides he needs some show for the expense account."

They all laughed, so I laughed, too.

"Well listen, man," Paco said, "I gotta drop these jokers off. Uh, you can hang out in front of the gas station and try to flag down a truck. See you later, huh?"

We shook hands and went outside. They piled in the truck and waved, pulling out on the highway and heading south. I moseyed along the road, watching the pickup, thinking, okay Jack, I'll check out Chorillo at eight in the morning. There'd be lots of cool things to do, like maybe buy a stamp at eight thirty, when the post office opened.

Damn, almost fell into some luck, I thought, Ramirez being a foreman and all—that could have been a job. And he had an expense account. Not too shabby. I popped my fist against my palm. Walking past the gas station, I kicked at the gravel and whistled one of those aimless stone-kicking melodies, y'know, random notes like a bouncing rock.

There was a loud piercing whistle. "Hey!" Yeah, I heard 'em. I looked around. I should have kept right on walking and kicking the stones, that'd have solved it all. "Hey you. You in the tramp suit." Two cowboys got up from a bench next to the Dr Pepper machine.

I looked at my brown rawhide jacket and my bluejeans and my black combat boots. "Say ... I don't think you gentlemen are whistling at me. Uh, must be some mistake," I said, knowing damn well otherwise. Stay alive long enough and you learn to smell an attitude. These boys had an attitude.

The taller man, who looked to be about my height, pushed his hat back. He had no eyebrows. He might have had blond hair but the crewcut was so short you couldn't tell. His eyes were like two black-brown beads. "I think this one's got hisself a mouth," he said to his friend.

When the second man's face emerged from shadow, I saw the vein-popped nose of an alky and the eye bags and fatty bulges of a beer drinker slowly oozing into middle age. He looked at me carefully, like he was gauging me or maybe memorizing my face, then he spit a stream of puke-brown tobacco on the ground. "Let him 'lone, Blaine," he muttered.

Blaine licked his lower lip, then grinned a sharp-tooth grin. "You a friend of Paco's, tramp man?" I told Blaine I didn't like his tone of voice. "Well, how-de-doo. How do you want me to talk to you, asshole, like your mother?" He started talking in a pip-squeak sort of voice. I leaned against one of the gas pumps and noticed a tire tool next to the air hose. The might be a nice just-in-case. With my buck knife in one hand and the tire tool in the other I thought I stood a fair chance of creasing both these boys, if it came to that. But I didn't want it to come to that.

I felt the first beads of sun sweat prickling my forehead.

"So what chew doin' with old Paco?" the shorter man asked, moving a wad of tobacco from one cheek to the other.

"I met the guy an hour ago. Why do you give a shit?"

The pudgy man sort of shrugged. "You just movin' through?"

"As long as the road ain't blocked."

"Where you headed?"

"New Mexico—unless I find me a job before then. You men don't know anything about any work around here, do you?"

The pudgy man spit again, then looked at Blaine. "We got any sort of em-ployment opportunities 'round here, Blaine?" Blaine rubbed his jaw, looked at me—looked at me hard—then said a nasty-sounding naw, a mean kind of no, as he sat back on the bench and brought his cowboy hat down over his eyes.

A boy of fifteen or so emerged from the station's repair bay. He had a half-dozen grease splotches on his face, and his hands were dirt black. "Can I help you, mister?" the kid asked, bright and friendly like.

"You gawn back and fix my Buick, Kirt. This fella's just

passin' through," the pudgy man told the boy. The kid gave the man a yes sir, put some change in the Dr Pepper machine, and got a can of soda. He went back in the bay as the alky-faced cowboy sat down and spat once more.

I took a chance. "The kid need any help? I've worked as a mechanic."

"You got the wrong impression, friend," the pudgy man replied, "iffn you think I own this place."

"Bennet don't own nothin'," Blaine said from beneath his hat.

The tobacco chewer grinned a sickly sort of fat-faced grin. "Now Ba-laine, I own a real nice Buick."

Blaine snorted. "You act like it's a Cadillac."

Bennet looked like he'd been spurred. "It could easily be a Cadillac," he said hotly.

"You're a chickenshit drunk," Blaine said as he folded his arms across his chest and leaned back like a taut spring imitating a relaxing man.

Bennet gave Blaine an angry, squinty-eyed stare. He pursed his lips, then his face blanched like a man who'd thought snake but then remembered poison. He cleared his throat and glanced at me. "Have fun in Nuevo Mexico, y'heah?"

I said sure, thanks. A huge rig was highballing down the blacktop. I grabbed my pack and jogged away from the pump, intending to flag the truck, and I tried—dammit, I really tried—but the eight-axle job just roared by. So I hiked past the Bar-B-Q shack and the next building, one that looked like a shut-down dance hall, and I planted myself beneath the first scrub tree that had a hat's worth of shade. I sat down and thumbed through a pocket Spanish dictionary I'd found in the rest room of a gas station in Houston. Might as well exercise the Spanish a little. I was never that good with the language, but I wasn't that bad either.

I brushed up under the scrub bush for close to three hours, and the only things that passed on the highway were a ten-year-old girl on a bike with training wheels and a Studebaker going in the wrong direction. My throat scratched—I was getting a hyper-thirst, so I walked back to the gas station, Blaine and Bennet weren't around, which was a plus, but Bennet's Buick was still in the repair bay. I had checked as I bought myself a Seven-up. "Hey, Kirt," I asked the boy mechanic, "who owns this joint?"

"Mr. Archibald."

I took a swig from the can of soda and washed it around in my mouth. "Where's Archibald hide himself?"

"Next door," the boy replied, as he crawled back under the car. "He's making bar-becue." I said thanks and went over to the concrete house. My stomach growled. Good, I thought, food time anyway, and the rich smell now emanating from the door of the Bar-B-Q post office convinced me I didn't want any more French toast or frijoles from La Fiesta. Besides, I'd just get all frustrated looking at Doreta's calves and knowing she was an impossible dessert.

Banging open the screen door, I walked into the concrete shack. Mesquite smoke wet the eye and smeared the bricked walls and the pine chairs with an oily veneer. A large, fat black man with two gold teeth in his upper gum, the only teeth in his upper gum, let loose a bassoon whoop. He stood beside a huge red-brick oven, rotating a rare chunk of hindquarter, looking like the Congo's version of Satan swabbing fat pink slabs of sinners and thoroughly enjoying this hell's fires.

"Get cho-self a plate," he said, raising an index finger, then jabbing it toward a pile of plastic cups and paper plates. I obliged. I handed him a plate and he slapped a piece of white bread on it, then drowned the bread in red juice and brown meat. "Pay the wife," he said, as he turned back toward his pit.

A tiny gray-haired woman with a thin lined face came out of the back and opened up a metal box that sat on a plywood table. "That's two seventy-five," she told me.

"Can I get something to drink?"

"Ice tea come with it."

There was another plywood table in the rear and I pulled up one of the el cheapo pine chairs and sat down. The woman brought me a tall glass of iced tea and a slice of lemon. She had a full set of teeth and looked to be a quadroon. She smiled and I asked her if the man by the oven was Mr. Archibald. "Yup," she replied. I took a big bite of the barbecue and half-drained the iced tea. "You like the food?" the old woman asked. I nodded. "Archie, he likes the food," she yelled, as she walked into the back.

"Good," Archie said with a voice that sounded like it began at the bottom of the earth.

"You own the gas station?" I asked.

He said yeah, but he didn't want me begging him about no job. As it was, business stank. "You better off moving on out. I hear there's still some jobs in Houston."

I told him I'd been through Houston and just about puked. "The smell man, all those petrochemicals," I said between thick bites.

Archie shrugged. "Sometimes bad smell means good money." He grinned and his two teeth shone like two small golden moons.

I got his message. "Yeah, but you're smelling bar-becue, not sulfur fumes."

He said that was the truth. "Where you from?" he asked.

I thought a moment. I could say Ponca City but a dude like Archie would have heard of it, so I said Detroit. "Detroit," he repeated. "You ever follow the Lions?" I said yeah, I followed football some. "You ever hear of Dwight Archibald?"

"Uh, yeah. Cornerback. The guy killed a couple of years back in an auto accident." Archie nodded. That was when I put the names together. "Gee, he wasn't your son was he?"

"Naw. A nephew."

"He was a damn fine player," I recalled. "First-round pick, wasn't he?"

Dwight Archibald had had a good rookie year and a couple of mediocre ones, then one damn fine all-pro season, so I remembered him, and I remembered reading about the accident. Apparently he'd been doing a lot of coke and the Chicago freeway he was driving on just wasn't big enough for both his car and his mind. Wham. One dead man and a lot of auto parts in critical condition.

"Hey, Martha," Archie called. "The white boy remembers Dwight."

The woman walked out of the back, mopping her face with a dirty washrag. "Wasn't he somethin' else?" she said, pouring me another glass of tea. She asked me where I was headed, and I decided to be honest and tell her I didn't really know. Had she heard of any jobs around? "In Chorillo?" she laughed. "Well, what can you do?"

I took another sip of tea. "I've been a mechanic, I've been a carpenter, I've even done some electrical work. if anybody needs anything, I ain't faking. I want a job so bad I can taste it."

"I don't rightly know." She shook her head. "We had a big storm a month back and folks are still fixin' up from that."

"Fixing what?"

"Houses. Fences. Cattle pens."

"I can do all that." I thought a moment. "Hell, I can even fly a helicopter." Boy, could I ever.

Her cream-colored face darkened. What'd I say? Her two large eyes became a pair of ice-brown pools and my paranoia level jumped a quantum. Naw, nobody around here could have heard about my piss-ant accident in Oregan. That hadn't amounted to a can of crap. But minds and paranoia make you think about such things. I got a twitch of the back shake.

Her face didn't help. She pursed her lips and waited a moment, like she was contemplating my face. "Say, friend," she said in a hard whisper, leaning toward me, "word to the wise—doan tell nobody 'round here you can *fly* anything."

"Huh? . . . How come?" That seemed like a logical kind of question.

"Just doan." She gave a pensive sort of frown and the crow's-feet around her eyes became an impenetrable web of age. Then she smiled. "Believe me, boy. I'm being Christian." She picked up the rag she'd been using to towel her face and wiped off the table. "If you can do electrical work, maybe you should move on up to Kerrville. They're putting in a *re-tire-ment* community near there," she called out loudly, looking in Archie's direction. She left the table.

So I dropped the subject of flying and pulled out my trusty road map. I found Kerrville. Hmmm. Now that did seem like a possibility. Yeah. Might take a couple of lucky rides, but it was certainly within a half-day's hitchhiking. "Will they give me any crap about being nonunion?" I asked Archie.

"What's that?" He moved out from behind his counter and away from the oven. I asked him about Kerrville and nonunion work. Sweat shone from his deep-bony skin like a reflective film of plastic. "Hey, boy, yo' in Texas. We got the right to work down here. All you got to do is hustle."

"I gotta hustle, huh. Like set me up a road stand and go in the bar-becue business?"

"Yeah. Why not," Archie grinned. "And get you a discount post office to boot."

I looked around the room. "Yeah. Well, where is the post office?"

Archie pointed to the metal change box. "In there. We also keeps the stamps in a drawer. They're the best-tasting lick in the entire U.S. postal system." I had to ask him what they tasted like. Archie popped one of his fingers in his mouth. "Sweat and bar-becue," he said with a smile.

# 3

I STEPPED OUTSIDE THE barbecue shack, slipping a stamp into my wallet. Cousin Pete might be due a letter, if something came up.

Paco's truck was parked in front of the grocery store across the highway. Well, Paco had been a straight dude. I'd just say hello and buy some envelopes. Maybe Paco and Joe and Fernando still had some fence to fix, but that didn't seem too likely—they probably had a ranch full of aliens to help with that sort of thing. I felt my wallet. A few more weeks like this and I'd be willing to go to Mexico and try to get a job down there, picking beans or farming dope. I didn't care. Or maybe I'd answer one of those newspaper ads asking for men with pilot's skills. The post office boxes were always in New York or L.A., but you had to know the airfields were either in Libya or El Salvador. Naw, bean picking was a good alternative. I'd seen too much lead in Vietnam to risk my one life for thirty thousand bucks a year, if that much.

Paco dropped an armload of wire and a sack of nails in the back of his pickup. "Still hanging around, huh, Buchanan?"

"Yeah. Nothin's coming down this highway."

"Guess I could have told you that. I could take you back up to San Diego or Benavides. It's easy to get a ride out of Diego."

"That'd be real nice."

"Couldn't do it 'til tomorrow morning."

I said thanks and if I couldn't catch anything during the afternoon, I might try and check him out. I scratched my nose and looked at the cloudless sky. The high-pitched whir of cicadas filled the air. I felt my boots against the hot asphalt and gravel, and it was getting hotter, all around. One could almost hear the heat.

"You won't catch anything, Buchanan. Around here the whole world's in siesta." Taking off his John Deere gimme cap, he moved his jet black hair off his forehead.

"If it gets hotter, I guess folks just don't move, huh," I remarked. "Sure wouldn't want to get paid by the hour having to work in this heat."

"Hmmm," Paco said. "It's not so bad."

"Still," I continued, following him into the store, "if I were working around here, I'd try to get going real early in the morning, or even work at night."

Paco smiled. "Well, hoss, around here a lot of folks do."

Inside I helped him pick up three boxes of roofing tiles and some more wire, both straight and barbed. We made a couple of trips. I went back inside and got a cold Dr. Pepper out of the store's cooler. I had to wait while the old woman behind the counter finished scratching her arm. "Forty cents," she said. She looked at me carefully. "You working with Paco now?" I said no. "Oh. Well, I thought you might be. Too bad. That woman's got plenty of money. She must pay him real good."

"What woman's that?"

The old lady clicked her false teeth. "The one that owns the place." Then the phone rang and she said wait a second. I took a big swig of DP and Paco came back in.

"Hey, Buchanan. You want to pick up some fast change?"

"You know it."

Paco stooped over and grabbed a can of creosote and another sack of eight-penny finishing nails. "I can use some help for the next few days. My, uh, extra hands had to split."

"Joe and Fernando."

"Yeah."

"What happened? They get sick on those Mexican eggs?"

"Naw. They got in a car and left and the stuff's not worth going into, believe me. You wanta work or do you want to bullshit?"

I took one last armload of wire and Paco nodded for me to grab a six-pack of Dos Equis beer. "Let's go. Hey, Mildred, put it all on the bill."

The stringy-haired old lady nodded an okay and continued to listen on the phone. "That's ten pounds of sugar?" she said into the receiver.

Paco drove about a mile and a half down the highway, then turned off onto a gravel tracked road. "You got a driver's license, Billy?"

"Sure."

"Good. Then you watch close. Not that this road is so damn difficult, but if you had to drive it at night, it can get tricky. Always better to do your recon with the light on, huh air scout?" I said yeah, usually, and sunk back in my seat.

Paco must have been the first Mexican I'd ever seen who didn't have a glow in the dark plastic Jesus hanging from his rearview mirror or a magnetized face of the Virgin stuck to the ashtray. What he had was a fancy, air-conditioned cab with a high-tech stereo and CB. "How come you don't have a CB aerial?" I asked.

He tapped the windshield. "Aerial's in there. If you want extra range, you do this." He pushed a button and a whip antenna telescoped from the hood.

I reached over my shoulder and rapped the rear window. "So howcome there's no gun rack in this truck? I thought every pickup in Texas was issued a gun rack by the state legislature."

Paco grinned. "Who needs a gun? Sounds like you've been reading too much propaganda."

The truck bounced over a couple of ruts, rattling my laziness. I checked out the lay of the land. Scrub oak, prickly pear, a scape of jagged flatness, dust brown earth and rock-red breaks cut by gullies. We crossed a bridge over a creek of dust. "Quivara Creek," Paco said. "It runs after every hurricane."

"Pretty dry around here?"

Paco shook his head. "No, not really. Lots of little creeks and springs, but a bunch of them start drying out this time of year. And we got some spit-size salt lakes south of here. One of them's pretty big though—Laguna Salada?"

I said I'd never heard of it, then changed the subject. "So Joe and Fernando and I are gonna stick up some fence?"

Paco made a hard turn on the wheel and I pitched forward. He drove the truck fast, the long trail of dust kicking off the rear tires like hot brown smoke. "No, you're going to help me. Fernando and Jose work in San Antone. Didn't I say they'd split?"

"They drive to San Antonio?" I asked. He said yeah, did I expect them to dance. I didn't know what to expect, I told him, but for me, Joe and Fernando could have been a ride to an interstate. "Guess I missed that boat, didn't I?"

Paco glanced at me. "Yeah. I hadn't thought about asking them to give you a ride."

"Heck, they could have dropped me off at a bus stop."

"Guess you blew that one, too. Texas Coach stops at the gas station at seven twenty-eight in the A.M. and splits at seven twenty-nine."

"While I was munching my toast." I sounded sort of sullen.

"Man, what do you want? You got a free ride and a free meal and now you got a job out of it. Maybe for a couple of weeks. This dust ain't gonna kill you."

So I perked up and said the job business sounded better and better. "What's the pay, anyway?"

Paco slowed the truck down. We were crossing another bridge, then we bumped over a cattle guard. "How's forty a day sound, including weekends? And you'll get Sundays off 'cause I'm against working on the Sabbath."

My jaw dropped. "Two hundred eighty a week?"

"That's what it sounds like."

"Off the books?"

"Man, you talk like you'd shoot a gift horse in the mouth. Naw, it's on the books."

Well, I didn't care if the IRS took a bite out of the pie. After all, I was once again getting something to chew on, and big bucks as far as I was concerned. Well, that was a lot of money for odd-jobbing, but hadn't I told Paco I could do electrical work and all? Maybe I could hide out down here, doing this and that, until the economy started turning up. Yeah.

Paco said something about how he'd forgotten to get some more gas. My mind returned to the gas station. "Hey, Pock. You know a couple of cowboys named Bennet and Blaine?"

He looked at the road, which was good because he just managed to avoid the butt of one very slow cow. "Sure do. They work on the Dickson place, next door to ours. You'll get to see some Dickson land when we fix fence."

Paco didn't seem to have anything further to say, so I dropped the subject. But I was wrong. "Where'd you meet Bennet?" he asked, his voice very upbeat.

"In the gas station. He and Blaine asked me about you."

A small grin cut a corner out of Paco's mouth. "Wasn't that nice of them," he said.

The road took a hairpin turn and wound up a rock-broken ridge. There were absolutely no clouds and the sun shone so bright it cast an almost milky glow to the afternoon land. We barreled through a couple of cattle guards, over a mesalike rise, then onto a straight stretch with a line of live oak. We stopped and I got out and opened a gate. Paco drove on through. Ten minutes later the road looped toward what Paco called "the spread." "Ranch house," he said, pointing out the obvious.

Mansion's more like it, I thought.

# 4

I SHOULD HAVE GUESSED the woman was rich and young and beautiful, as in cool, with exacting taste and class. The white Mercedes sports coupe tipped me off, then the calculated sunglasses and those long, mean legs below the tight white jogging shorts made it a certainty. I wanted to see her eyes, but the ultraban shades hid them behind hard lids.

"Who's he, Paco?" she demanded, as she walked from the ranch house door to her car. She carried a cane purse that on a second look was shaped like a rattan armadillo.

"His name's Billy," Paco replied, getting out of the truck.

I just stayed in the pickup's shotgun seat and let my imagination do its thing. My eyes checked her blouse. Maybe medium in the chest, and then came her strong, hard chin and a set of firm lips. I closed my eyes. Yeah, I'd seen her kind before, your Playmate with a rich-bitch T-shirt. Damn. And her kind of class was out of my league. I didn't have any money or any M.B.A. Now maybe I wasn't so bad-looking in a tough kind of way and, besides, girls were always saying that a lot of the delicate handsome types were really bores. Yeah, I had some personality to me, but there wasn't any real use in kidding around. The movie starlet rich-girl world was well beyond my grab, not that my fingers wouldn't try. Did I care? I thought a moment. Shit, I guess the housewife and saleswoman were good enough for me and, thank God, they probably had damn fewer hangups, unless the woman was a chick computer expert. You always got to watch the ones that move around electricity and numbers. Naw, all in all my heart went with the working girl.

I opened my eyeballs. She was looking toward me, coolly, sizing me up, mantis-like, from behind her dark green blinders. Okay, lady, I thought, yeah I'm beneath you honey, but from down here you sure have a nice beneath. You're beautiful and you're a snob and I'm halfway in stupid love. Oh Lord, did I have the urge to touch her, and she knew it 'cause I could feel the icy blast from behind those shades. She got in her sports car, waved goodbye to Paco, backed it out of the drive, and drove off.

"What's her name?" I asked Paco, as he climbed back in the truck.

"Elaine Masterson."

"She a Miss or Ms?"

"Down here Missus always sounded like Miz. Progressive neighborhood, huh?" He raised an eyebrow. "Why don't you just call her Miz Masterson and forget about anything else."

"Anything else?"

Paco nodded and said yeah. He didn't grin.

I looked back at her house, or rather her ranchified mansion. Two stories, a brick bottom and a wooden upstairs with a porch—a new build on an old farmhouse. I knew that took some cash. Paco turned onto another gravel road, which looped around the house, and I saw a swimming pool in back and the lush green lawn spreading out in long arcs from a series of permanent sprinklers. There was a little cabana down from the pool.

The road bent through a short draw, then came out beside a long white rail fence running past a one-story frame house and leading to a huge white barn. "That's the bunkhouse, Billy. We got blankets and the works in there." I felt around my face, scratching the two-day growth of beard. Paco noticed—he had a detailed eye. "I've got an extra razor if you want it. Why don't you take a shower. I'm gonna run up to the fence site and pick up a pair of posthole diggers. The house key's hidden under the barrel cactus, second planter to the left of the door."

The bunkhouse divided into five rooms, a living room backed by a kitchenette, a hall that passed a room with two bunk beds, one with a pair of twin beds, then a room with a single—that one must be Paco's since it was the only one in use. After I checked out the pad, I put the six-pack in the refrigerator and went to the bathroom. It had two shower stalls and two basins.

The shower and shave really set me straight. I hadn't known how dirty I was until I washed the mud off the shower's tile floor. Given the gritty residue, I must have been well on my way to being a set of bones with soot for skin.

I walked into the kitchen wearing a pair of shorts and nothing else. The beer was still a little warm but I latched on to it, then turned on the TV. Only one channel came in with any clarity and I decided I didn't want to watch a sick little soap opera about horny nurses and impotent New York doctors.

Elaine kept clawing her way back into my brain and I thought that I just might offer to hire myself out to her as some kind of love slave. I took a sip of warm beer. But naw, I said, you better forget her, she's too boss. I shook my head. I couldn't forget that body. Elaine was the best-looking woman I'd seen since the redhead in Nevada. Now what was that casino girl's name? Christine? Christina? Yeah, something like that.

I got out another warm beer as Paco walked in. No, he didn't want one, it was too hot, the weather and the beer, and, speaking of heat, why in God's name hadn't I turned on the air conditioner? He went to the window and turned on the blower and in about forty-five seconds I was starting to get some nice goose bumps. The chill felt good.

Paco and I made some ham sandwiches and talked. "I'll show you around some this evening, Bill. Tomorrow you can show me if you really know anything about running fence and hammering nails. You're going to end up working here by yourself some so you'd better not cross me, y'heah, and act like you're thinking about taking something." He looked at me with a steel sort of wink in his eye. "You follow me, Buchanan?" he asked.

I just grinned. "I've never stolen much of anything in my whole life."

"Okay," Paco said, giving his teeth a quick clench. "Just don't start now. I'm hiring you because you look like you can work and you act halfway honest."

Heck, I thought, I am honest. Then I stopped for a second. No, the only thing I'd ever really stolen, outside of stealing from the army, and of course that didn't count, was that six-pack of Cokes I swiped from a neighborhood kid in Ponca City who'd gone and bragged to everybody that he'd shoplifted the drinks. Stealing from a thief wasn't really stealing, was it? Why, it might even be a crude kind of justice—that'd been my rationalization then and it still seemed pretty good now. That kid's loud mouth had done him in, too. He'd gotten caught by his parents and he couldn't cough up the goods. His old man just blistered his butt. Well, I told the kid later, you got to learn to keep your mouth shut and cover your tracks, and next time you got a rock don't throw it at Aunt Doe's car, you understand. Yeah, Don had a tendency to hurl stone missiles at old women in Chevys, a tendency my fist began to discourage.

"Hey, Pock," I said after another sip of beer, "you're a damn fine judge of manpower."

That evening we took a drive while the sun took its time going down. A breeze blowing from the east, all the way from the Gulf, Paco said, cooled down the local world. We stopped by a pile of posts and Paco pointed out a staked twenty-by-twenty-foot square. "That's gonna be a small holding pen," he indicated. "We've got a tractor with a drill screw to do the rough work, but you'll have to finish off the holes with good ole back muscle."

We drove back to the bunkhouse, finished off the six-pack, and Paco went to sleep. I watched a Marlon Brando flick about motorcycles, then turned in.

We woke early, like around five or so, and Paco and I split a half dozen eggs. "These eggs come off my forty bucks a day?" I asked, cramming a piece of toast in my mouth. Paco shook his head and continued to chew. "Man," I said lightly, "we must be sucking off one rich tit." Paco looked up at the ceiling and shook his head. "Why'd you do that?" I asked. He took a swig of coffee and told me to worry about eating and to forget about budgets and tits.

I should have worried about postholes in rocky soil, not to mention red scorpions and mosquito hordes lurking in the mesquite. And the sun, I should have worried about the sun. Thank God for the Texaco gimme hat Paco tossed me as we were leaving the bunkhouse. "It's Joe's," he said, "but he won't miss it. Texaco didn't when he took it from them."

Paco filled an Igloo water cooler and got a Styrofoam box and iced down some Cokes and DPs. "No beer?" I asked.

"You wanta throw up?" he replied. He dropped in a can of Seven-up.

We drove out to a long low-back ridge that rose out of a series of sand and prickly pear–clustered dunes. The truck crunched through an empty draw, breaking over gravel stones the size of horse teeth and white as old bone. Paco turned up another dirt track, switching the truck to four-wheel drive as we skirted a thick stand of mesquite. The limb of a scrub oak snapped through my rolled-down window and scratched the hell out of my cheek.

"Shit," I said, "you should have warned me."

Paco replied with a grin. "You shoulda been thinking. That chinery and mesquite can be nasty stuff."

"Chink what?" I asked.

"Chinery. Scrub oak. Same thing 'cept different words. Now keep your eye on that ridge. That's where we'll be working the fence line on and off for the next week or so." His head gave an up-tick. "The Dickson Ranch is just on the other side."

We parked by a stack of wooden fence posts. The tractor with the posthole screw stood beside a large mesquite. I pulled the posthole diggers out of the back of the truck while Paco went over to the tractor and mounted up. "I'm going to head up top. A lot of the holes down here are in, you sharpen them up. Just follow the old fence line. And watch out for snakes." He winked.

He should have said watch out for barbed wire. Within five minutes I'd torn a nice slice in my blue jeans. Well, that's why Sears gave me an extra pair, I said, keeping up the sense of humor. By noon I must have sucked down three gallons of water and shed four. It went on like that for a couple of days, up in the mornings, out to the ridge, busting them holes. We finished most of the holes and planted in a couple of hundred yards of post.

Then one morning Paco didn't wake me at five. I rolled out of my bed and had that fuzzy eyeball feeling that sets in after too much sleep. The clock on the stove said eight forty-five and no, ole Paco wasn't in his bed or in the shitter. I shaved—I'd gotten in the habit of shaving again, since I was making money—got a cup of coffee, then stepped out of the house when I heard a car driving up the road.

Paco and a tough-looking man with sunglasses—short blond hair, medium build—got out of a beige Ford sedan, a car with blackwall tires. "Hey," I yelled, "today ain't Sunday is it?" I yawned and scratched my bare chest. It wasn't nine, yet a nice blast of noon was already in the breeze. The guy with the sunglasses, who wore a blue three-piece polyester suit and seemed to do so without sweating, asked Paco who I was.

"That's Billy," Paco replied. "Thought I mentioned him. He's helping out on the fence." Three-Piece Suit nodded and got back in the car. "Punch the trunk button," Paco shouted, as he moved to the rear of the car. I saw the guy with the sunglasses lean across the seat and comply. The trunk lid popped up and Paco pulled out a carbine, M-1 type. He brought me the rifle, then handed me a couple of ammo clips. "I'm going to San Antonio for a couple of days," he said, "and that's for snakes. Foreign and domestic."

I brought the bolt back and checked the chamber. "I haven't seen any snakes," I said.

"Then use it on big scorpions," Paco replied.

"I thought you said we didn't have any guns around here." I must have been grinning.

"Well, don't believe everything you hear. Besides, this is Texas, isn't it? Didn't you tell me everybody up North says we're armed to the teeth?"

"Hey, I was born in Dalhart, up in the Panhandle. I grew up in Oklahoma. I know what a gun is."

"Dalhart? That's so far north it may as well be Yankee." Paco slapped me on the shoulder.

"Well, a shotgun would be better if I ran into a snake."

"Keep the carbine," Paco said.

"Wouldn't a pistol be handier, 'specially if I'm using a set of posthole diggers?" I made a motion like I was digging a hole and my shoulder muscles twinged. I hadn't realized I was sore.

"Keep the carbine," Paco repeated. "Who knows, the ranch might get attacked by poachers or javelina and you'll have to defend it."

"Wild pigs?"

Paco snorted like a boar and walked back to the Ford.

"What do you want me to work on?" I asked.

Paco got in the car and rolled down the window. "Stick in a few more posts up on the ridge, then get to work on that pen I showed you. And there's another new pen going in down in the southwest corner. It's been staked. Here." He took a pad of paper off the car seat, got a pen from Three-Piece Suit, and sketched a map. "It's already laid out. Put the holes in. If you can finish all that before I get back, you can get drunk for all I care. The keys are in the truck and don't you even think of stealing it and splitting for, where, Wisconsin?" He said Wisconsin with a kind of leading tone, like he was trying to trap me.

"Michigan," I said. "And what'll happen if I do?"

Paco made a slicing sound and brought the chop of his hand across his throat. "Plan on picking me up at Mildred's next Satuday around noon, okay?"

"Mildred's?"

"Millie's. The grocery store in Chorillo?"

"Oh yeah."

Paco gave me the map.

I got out to the ridge about ten fifteen and worked till

one, when I took a siesta in the cab of the truck. I woke up at three, with a tarantula crawling like a hairy cloud across the windshield. I knocked the dark thing off the glass—I don't know how it could have stood the heat— and went back to work, stringing a little straight wire and sinking posts until seven, knocked off, went back to the bunkhouse, took a shower, and got me a drink.

Now I don't drink too much and I don't drink too often, but I've drunk enough to know that different breeds of booze hit me in different ways. Scotch puts me to sleep. A couple of shots of Irish whiskey usually leads to a fight. Gin gets me sick. And tequila, well, tequila makes my head hum, or buzz—buzz in a low, soft key—and then it can lead anywhere, to a snooze, to a fistfight, to another bar. Paco had a bottle of tequila laid aside and I poured a couple of shots, drinking them slow, getting just a little buzz, not drinking enough to nod off and not slipping in the direction of a fight either. I'm not in the habit of fight- ing with myself, absolutely not. In other words, I'm not a psychologist or a preacher.

I watched the tail end of another Brando flick, this one about a white horse in Mexico, then downed a third shot of tequila. It'd been another long day, so no way was I gypping Paco or Miz Tight-Ass Masterson, at least as I saw it. Well, maybe Paco hadn't intended for me to find that bottle of tequila hidden under the sink, but then he didn't know I'd spill a can of Wolf brand chili and need some cleanser. Sometimes you can find a treasure when you're not even looking for it.

So I couldn't sleep—the buzz was too nice—and I didn't want to sleep and I opened the bunkhouse door. Out on the porch the first rush of Gulf breeze slapped me near sober. I took a walk. No lights were on up at the ranch mansion—the Miz had bolted for Houston—so sex, real or imagined, didn't enter into the picture. Give it up, boy, I thought. You just don't have her kind of class.

Then I looked up at the sky and it seemed that this was the first time I'd ever really seen the sky, at least since I was a kid in Ponca City. The light, the very noise of Detroit and Pontiac seemed to shut out the stars, and in Lansing, well, I'd worked too hard in Lansing. I turned my head. Above me were thousands of stars, strings and clusters, loners, hard bits of unblinking stone-white ice in the cloudless air. I knew a couple of names, but the only name I could match for sure was the Big Bear, the constellation of the North Star. I found it. Christ, I could have been a Boy Scout.

Off in the distance to the west and south I thought I heard the yelp of a dog, a wild sort of yelp, a yelp that turned into a long, low moan. A coyote? Maybe he'd found some chickens to chase. I walked back to the barn and wandered around to the far side. An aluminum extension ladder lay beside the barn wall, and suddenly I had an itch on my ass. I pulled the ladder out to max length and set it against the barn. It just reached the lowest dip of the roof, and with a little care I climbed up and managed to get my belly over the gutter, dangle my legs, and crawl onto the top of the barn.

The stars didn't look any different, but the land did. I thought I could see, way to the north, a bare line of light. San Antonio. Paco was probably getting down in some fast-paced bar. Yeah, I'd have to give S.A. a chance sometime, a chance to take my money. To the east and a little north I saw a low glowing dome. Corpus Christi, maybe, burning the midnight oil. To the south and west I saw only what the moonlight reflected, with the exception of what seemed to be a distant radio tower with a winking red light and a couple of uncertain, unblinking lights that had to be farmhouses.

The coyote had stopped barking. I clambered up to the top of the tin roof and sat down, just watching the land and feeling the breeze. Why couldn't Texas save some of this cool air for noontime? Well, the Mexicans had the right idea—sleep at noon.

I thought I had a real good view of nothing and I liked the view and I liked the air.

Back toward the northwest I followed the wavering lights of what must have been a truck heading south or southeast on some highway. Well, there were other humans out and moving. Over to the west toward one of the faint houselights—it seemed not so far away, but then the distances in clear night air fool even former pilots—another headlight came on, then flicked off. Somebody trying to start a car? I coughed and started to slide back down the roof. My tequila buzz had worn off, but the move over the gutter would be a trick even if I was stone sober in broad daylight.

More lights came on, headlights spaced apart or so it seemed, like a car lot in that far valley, which must have been miles beyond our property. Our property? Why did I say that? Miz Masterson owned this joint, didn't she? I didn't own anything except a short-term job.

The headlights stayed on for a couple of minutes. Then went off, one set, a couple of more, then the last. All dark again—and the coyote started another long moan. Eventually I made it down the ladder and back into bed.

The next morning I was out early and I finished the first corral, at least from the empty hole point of view. I could see that Paco and I had a lot of work ahead of us if we were going to do it all ourselves. About two o'clock I drove back to the bunkhouse and had lunch, then got out the map Paco had drawn.

It took me nearly three hours of tracking, backtracking, spinning tires out of ruts, and just general wild-ass guessing to find the second corral, or pen. Christ, closet would have been more accurate, a fenced-in closet. It looked to me like the thing was three-quarters finished, with a couple of aluminum posts set in concrete and sunk about six feet apart, but then there were a half-dozen stakes and twine running around the whole area, so I did have some work to do.

The two posts set in concrete looked sort of like gate-posts, but they were in an odd place for a gate—directly over a six-inch drop that broke into a wide treeless space that rolled down into a long scooped-out valley, a valley that shot back arrowlike toward the south but seemed to broaden as it ran north. Mesquite and scrub oak darkened in the valley's bottom as its rim reflected the sinking sun's reddening waves. I started digging, knowing I was going to have to work my butt off if I didn't want to get lost in the dark. A night trip back to the bunkhouse wouldn't be fun.

I dug out the first hole—the soil was like a piece of bed-rock and I had to twist the digger's spades double hard—and started on the second, but the night was winning the race. So I just relaxed, slapped a mosquito off my fore-head, and decided to take my time. I could always cut on the truck's headlights if I needed work light.

I took a break and found a Seven-up in the Styrofoam cooler. Paco'd been right—a man had to avoid beer in this heat. I picked up the soft drink. All the ice in the cooler had melted, but the water was still cold to the touch. I drained the can, then thought it'd be wise to get my rifle out, just in case of any unwanted night life. I moved my carbine off the passenger's seat, then, on an impulse, found a flashlight in the truck's glove compartment, along with a .357 Magnum revolver. Okay, Paco, I thought, somebody's kidding somebody. I put the pistol back in the glove compartment, flicked on the flashlight, and went back to the pen, leaning my rifle against one of the metal posts. It was late twilight, near dead dark.

A low, increasingly intense thrum, the roar of airplane

engines, rolled up the valley. From the south. I moved to the edge of the drop. Like a huge black sound, a gigantic bat, the plane shot up the valley, hugging the scrub oak, all dark, with no lights.

Whaa? The dumb suck's gotta get his lights on, I thought. The loud wrang of nearing piston engines reached its peak, then disappeared in a long bending throb.

The fucker's too low, I thought, way too low. Shit, I could fly the nap of the earth in a copter, but in a big twin-engine plane, so low, at twilight, with a half moon barely on the rise?

Well, maybe it wasn't all that dark. But no lights? That shook my pilot's fiber.

I heard the sound of the plane banking in the distance. I couldn't tell which way the turn was going, but there was a grab for altitude.

Some army test? Air force? Bullshit. I really didn't think that. Why play dumb, 'cept for continuity's sake? Naw. I'm not so stupid. A north-south valley with the south-end butt stuck in Mexico? Don't have to be Einstein to answer that one.

# 5

I WAS FILLING THE truck up at the Source Oil Company, Gasoline Marketing Division—putting it on the bill like young Kirt said—when I heard Paco shouting. He was already in front of Millie's. I checked my watch—not even near noon, just five after eleven. I hadn't noticed a truck or car stop, but then I'd been in the back of the station shooting the breeze with Kirt and Archie for almost a half hour.

I stopped pumping gas. "What'd you say?" I yelled.

Paco shouted back and told me to get my ass down there as soon as I finished. I topped off the tank and hollered to Kirt and Archie. "Hey, boy," Archie called, as I started the truck, "we be seein' you, huh?" I just waved as I rolled the truck out on the highway and cruised to the grocery.

Paco was back in the store, talking to an old, and I mean *old* woman. She was built like a short, muscled refrigerator, and she wore an Indian shawl and a pair of turquoise earrings. Her braided, piled hair was ash gray, ash the color of cold fire embers, and her eyes were two small black dots.

"Si, si," Paco was saying, as I entered, then he let go another paragraph or two of Spanish, all fired out in about four seconds. He bent over and gave the woman a kiss on the cheek.

She reacted, but almost imperceptibly.

"This is my amigo, Billy," Paco said.

I said howdy. She moved her two black eyes toward me and nodded. "Buenos dias," she said. Yeah, I understood that. Then she said something to Paco. He held the door for her and she stepped out, moving slowly and methodically.

"Who is she?" I asked.

Paco went over to the cooler and got a beer. "People call her great-grandmother," he said, twisting off the beer top. "You want one of these?"

"Not if we're gonna be working," I replied.

"You learn fast, muchacho, but who said anything about work. Gotta re-lax sometime." He tossed me a brew as Millie came out from the back of the store and said something about loud boys throwing things inside houses. Paco slapped a dollar by the cash register.

"Is she a great-grandmother?" I asked.

"Who, Madre?" Paco took a sip of beer and nodded. "For some folks more than others."

I glanced out the window. Bennet's blue Buick had stopped and the old lady was getting into the car. Bennet wasn't driving and the man in the seat sure wasn't Blaine. I didn't recognize the driver—he was a cowboy wearing a powder blue shirt.

"She work at the Dickson place?" I asked.

"Yeah," Paco replied as he swished beer from cheek to cheek. "The lady's a real interesting character. Folks say she was a lover of Villa's."

"Pancho Villa?"

"No. Donald McDonald Villa. Of course Pancho Villa. Who else is Villa when someone says Villa?" He feigned disgust.

I finished my beer and gave off with an oh wow. "Is it true?"

Paco thought a minute, then went over and picked up a Kripax fried pie. "It's true enough." He opened the cellophane wrapper and downed the pie in two bites, then licked his fingers.

"My grandaddy was in the cavalry, down in Mexico chasing Pancho Villa," I said.

Paco said something like wrollf.

"Shouldn't talk while your mouth is full," Mildred interrupted. She was sweeping out the back of the store. "Eat like that young man and you'll choke to death. Don't pay me for the pie and you'll go to jail."

Paco swallowed. "So your grandpappy was off chasing Villa? What'd he catch besides a mouthful of dust?" He knocked the crumbs off his lip and got another beer.

"He sure as hell didn't catch a hot case of Mexican clap."

"Don't be so damn sure, gringo," Paco retorted. He went over to Millie and gave her another couple of bucks. "Your momma could have had syph zits on her face."

I smiled. "Well, I never saw my momma. You could be right."

Paco took another hit of beer and looked me square in the eyeballs. "Your grandaddy really chase Villa?"

I nodded. "Yeah, he really did. Before he died he always used to talk about getting to see the army's first plane. The Signal Corps had this scout craft they'd put up every so often."

"Didn't help, did it?"

"Naw," I said, "the plane never saw nothin'. Back then there were a lot of places to hide."

Paco started laughing. "There still are—fortunately and unfortunately . . ." He paused. "Hey, let's get out of here." He started toward the door and yelled good-bye to Millie.

We got in the truck and drove back to the ranch. By the Quivara Creek bridge we had to pull over to the side as a Jeep Wagoneer and a three-axle Ryder rental truck barreled across the one-and-a-half lane span. Dust and grit fogged the windshield, and I waited for the swirl to settle before inching back on the track and crossing the dry creek.

"Did'ja have a good time in San Antone?" I asked.

Paco said yeah, he always had a good time in S.A. I asked him if he'd seen Fernando and he started to shake his head no—then he said yeah. He looked distracted. "So how's Fernando's truck business?" I asked, making the hairpin turn and heading up the low ridge.

"Fernando doesn't drive a truck," Paco said.

We bumped over a cattle guard. "Gee, I thought he told me he did. What's he do?"

We pulled up to the first ranch gate. Somebody'd unlocked it and left it swinging half-open—somebody who had been out to the ranch since I'd driven into town. "He works somewhere," Paco finally said to me as he jumped out and held the gate. I drove through and he climbed back in the cab.

I quit asking about Fernando and no, I wasn't going to ask anything about Joe either, not after seeing last night's airplane. And the gate—I wondered who'd been through the gate.

"Well," Paco said, in a voice that sounded like it had just woke up from a long nap, "how'd the ranch business go? Things all nice and quiet?"

I thought about the airplane and the on-again, off-again lights, then I thought again, cut the truth into fourths, and told two of them. "I put in some posts. And I killed a tarantula."

"Heck, those spiders are harmless, they just look mean and hairy," Paco said.

Miz Masterson's Mercedes was parked in front of the ranch house. Well, guess that explains the gate. You'd expect the little rich brat to be thoughtless, not that she had that many cows to lose. I told Paco somebody ought to tell her not to leave the gates unlocked, and he told me to stuff it 'cause cows aren't going to step across cattle guards. "What do you think they're for?" he asked.

Elaine was lying beside the swimming pool, wearing an undersize bikini and an oversize pair of sunglasses. She stood up and waved as we drove around the side of the yard. Paco waved back.

I stopped the truck in front of the bunkhouse. Paco got out of the cab and slipped on an attaché case from beneath the seat. I hadn't seen him put it in and I asked him where he'd gotten it. Was it new? He shook his head from side to side. "Does it look new?" he asked, holding it up to my face. It was metal, beaten with dents and cut with scratches.

We both went inside the bunkhouse and Paco washed up. The doorbell rang. Elaine was at the door, her suntan-lotioned skin slick as a seal's. I let her in, then went back to the refrigerator. Checking out the way her tits stuffed that white bikini was just too much frustration for me to handle. I decided that I'd do myself a whole lot better if I occupied my mind with a ham and cheese on rye.

"A truck came by and dumped off a load of material," she told Paco. Hmm, I thought.

Paco said good as he toweled his face. "Where'd they store it?"

"By the barn. They put some bricks up by the house."

"Okay," Paco said, "we'll get on it."

I turned toward Elaine. "When are you going back to Houston?" I asked her.

She lowered the gaudy sunglasses, pushing them down

her nose, then peered at me, like I was a blob of dumb. "Shouldn't you be asking how long I'm going to stay?"

I guess I turned a little red. I didn't say anything else, except mutter a yeah, maybe, as I went back to the john. Christ, she was beautiful, and smartass smart.

Paco was putting on a pair of knee boots when I came back. I saw Elaine through the kitchen window, walking toward the house, her bikini bottom just barely keeping all that beautiful sashaying ass tucked in. "She get to you, hoss?" He asked with a grin.

I balled up my fist, then lightly tapped it against one of the kitchen cabinets. "Hell yes," I said. Paco laughed. I watched him. "Say, partner," I said, "you seem to keep pretty cool about her."

"Yeah," he replied, "and I practice at it. Professional respect. Get your boots on. I want to take some of the new stuff out to the new corral ... say, did you finish the little pen down on the southwest fence?"

I said I had. "Just had to dig three or four holes."

We found a pile of new posts, some pieces of aluminum siding, a box of nails, and some rolled tarp by the barn. Six sacks of concrete and a roll of wire lay next to the barn door. I brought the truck around and Paco set a couple of strips of siding in the back. I got out and started handing him posts. "Easy. Just toss in three or four. We'll get the rest later."

We drove out to the twenty-by-twenty corral and Paco liked the job I'd done, including sinking in the posts and lining up some slots for the siding. He mentioned that the delivery truck should have brought out a couple of gates and we'd put one up next week. I finished tossing out the posts and Paco put a sack of concrete underneath a tarp he'd stuck back in the brush.

"You did some work the last few days, Buchanan," he said.

"You're paying top dollar," I told him. I felt proud. "You want to drive out and see the Dickson fence line? I strung a long piece of it."

Paco thought a minute, then said naw, he was satisfied. If I said I'd finished that line, he believed me. "You really worked your ass off if you got all I asked for done. We'll just let the rest set 'til next week."

**6**

I HEARD A SLEDGE hammer pounding on the tin roof of my dreams, and then it stopped being a sledge hammer and became a doorbell. I checked my watch—7:30 A.M. Christ, I thought, rolling out of bed and going down the hall to get the door, a man can't even sleep late on Sunday. I glanced in Paco's room. He was in snooze city with a pillow crammed over his face.

The doorbell rang again. It was Elaine. Well heck, I thought, if she's got the gall to bust in here this early, she can just see me in a pair of jockey shorts. I didn't say anything to her when I opened the door. She wore a pair of brown riding breeches, a short-sleeve polyester shirt, and her mandatory sunglasses. She'd pulled her long brunette hair back into a bun. And it was obvious she didn't give a damn about my shorts.

"Coffee on?" she asked as she looked around the living room.

I tried to rub sleep out of my eyes.

She went to the kitchen range and started banging

around, looking for a pot. "Left-hand side," I said. "The cupboard."

Swinging the door open—and it slammed, nice and loud—she got the pot out and started filling it with water. "If you go and get dressed, you can go to the races," she said, not bothering to look at me. Then she turned and gave me an eye. "You seem like the kind of guy that likes horse races."

I rubbed my unshaven jaw. "I do like horse races," I replied, "if there's betting. And if the horses are fast."

"Then why don't you get dressed. I think we can meet or exceed both of your standards."

So I said okay, and went back into my room and pulled on a pair of jeans and boots and a brand-new pearl button cowboy shirt Paco had given me. He'd taken it out of his closet last night when he came back from the ranch house and said it was two sizes too big for him. "I think this was Fernando's," he said, "Why don't you wear it. Your clothes are ratty as hell." Though a little tight in the neck, the shirt fit me just about perfect.

I slopped some deodorant under my arms, knowing full well I'd sweat it off inside an hour, then went into the bathroom and shaved. When I came out, Elaine was draining a cup of coffee. "Did you make any for me?" I asked.

"Right here," she said, moving a steaming cup down the counter toward me. "You didn't think I would? What do you think I am?" So she asked me—what an opening.

I took a sip of coffee and looked at her. "Selfish," I said.

"Oh Christ." Her eyes rolled toward the ceiling.

"Presumptuous as all get out," I added.

She stared at me, her fingers drumming against the counter. "You got a fast mouth for an employee," she said, but she didn't say it meanlike, more as if she were merely making a statement of fact about the world.

So I shut up about reality and went for small talk. I told

her I didn't mind being ordered around to go to a horse race. But on a Sunday? "Besides," I added, "I know that betting on a horse race is illegal in Texas. Betting just ain't Baptist."

"Don't you have a lot to learn," she replied, glancing at her watch. "Well, are you going to escort me or aren't you?"

"This going to be professional or personal?"

She shrugged. "Don't you get paid for Sunday?"

I put the coffee cup down. "Why me instead of Paco?"

"You're up and he's asleep and Miz Masterson is in a hurry." She gave me a cold stare, a stare like distance itself.

A groan emerged from Paco's room. "Would you two get the hell out of here or shut the bullshit up, one or the other?" He let out a choice Spanish phase.

"Go back to sleep, you lazy Mex," Elaine yelled.

We walked out onto the porch. "Hey," I said, "can we go in the fast-class sports car of yours?"

"Sure. But I drive. You can ride shotgun."

"Gee. That's decent of you lady, seeing as there's only two seats."

We walked up to the ranch house and she looked at my sunburned face and told me that I ought to wear a hat and "not one of those grimy gimme hats either." She had the solution. I waited by the Mercedes while she went into her house and came back with a jet black ten-gallon Resistol. She gave the crown a rap, then popped the hat on my head.

The only time she bothered to slow down between the ranch and the highway was when we stopped because of the gate, and she was gunning it as soon as I got back to the passenger's door.

We turned onto Highway 16 heading north and she kept the pedal down. It didn't take us but another fifteen or twenty minutes of ninety plus to get to Freer, where she slowed down for a flashing yellow light. As she barreled through at fifty in a thirty-zone, she waved to the state cop sitting on the hood of his patrol car eating an ice cream cone. So much for Freer. She talked a little bit about Houston and I told her about my experience with the smog, sweat, and freeway gridlock and she said yeah, that was some of the reality, but there was a lot of other reality that contradicted that portion, and Houston was big and she just couldn't park permanent like down on a South Texas ranch. "The city has an energy, an excitement," she said, "you know what I mean?" I said that I thought I did.

We reached a small highway intersection and turned left. Three or four minutes later Elaine slowed down, to about seventy-five, then told me to look around for a white-brick fence.

"What about a white blur?" I asked.

But she was already slowing down, having seen the white-brick gate, an arch of stone breaking up the endless lines of barbed wire. A tall cowboy slouched against one of the pillars. He didn't glance twice as Elaine turned off the highway onto the gravel road, then down-shifted and flashed on by.

"A careful guardian at the gate," she muttered.

The road curved through stretches of scrub oak and mesquite. Gravel kicked up against the sides of the car. I thought about the high price of dents, but then I didn't own this Mercedes, she did.

The gravel became asphalt. The line of scrub and now live oak broke into a huge green irrigated meadow. Across a long stretch of manicured bermuda grass rose a three-story white-brick mansion. A string of Mercedes, El Dorados, Continentals, and El Caminos curved around the driveway, mixing with a variety of Jeep Cherokees, International Harvesters, and Dodge pickups.

Elaine found a spot and parked the car beneath a tree.

As we got out, a man of medium build, wearing a cowboy hat and carrying a Remington 12-gauge pump, walked up to us. "I'm Elaine Masterson," she said tartly. He tipped his hat, said howdy, then looked in a little black notebook he pulled from his front pocket. "Come on, Bill," she said to me.

The man with the shotgun didn't say anything else.

I could see a group of men and women in mixed dress, shirt-sleeves and suits, pantdresses and blue jeans, standing by the mansion's front porch. They drank and talked and laughed. A tall blonde, wearing a white halter top and a pair of white hot pants, waved to Elaine. Elaine waved back.

"Who's that?" I asked.

"Her name's Azure. She balls the old goat who owns this place."

"Oh," I replied. "It is some place."

"He's got one near Corsicana that's even bigger."

Elaine and I walked through a pecan grove and came out onto a grass-covered knoll. Three hundred yards to the north was a huge oval race track ringed by white rail fences, pin oaks, and spectators. From the distance it looked as if a part of Kentucky and a slice of Georgia had been levitated, submitted to strange mathematical permutations, then dropped flat-ass into the desert of South Texas. I said so. Elaine scowled. "This isn't any desert. The Nueces isn't more than two miles north of those stables." She pointed to a pair of long two-story wooden buildings with air conditioners stuck in every one of the barracks-like windows.

"Okay," I said. "It ain't a desert. I don't think it's a desert anyway. It's too wealthy."

And that was no lie. One of the finest Texas collections of scoundrels, high rollers, legislators, thieves, old money, odd money, new money, oil money, borrowed money, loafers, jawboners, poachers, gas station operators, blues singers, country fiddle players, cheats, tax lawyers, rustlers, special prosecutors, drillers, refiners, slant holers, roughnecks, rednecks, Yankees, daisy-chainers, and good ole boys and gals ever assembled coiled around the white track fence and mingled cozily beneath the tall, wide oak trees. And to hell with wine and champagne. Hard bourbon and dark rye flowed like luscious muddy water, slowly chugging downstream into the collective thirst. The blue jeans, Gucci shoes, Vuiton purses, Neiman's pantsdresses, handmade cowboy boots, Stetsons and hundred-dollar-a-collar western shirts made it very Texan, even if a good ten to fifteen percent of the accents were solidly New York faggot or Long Island twit and another good chunk of the populace were pseudo-Harlem hustlers, wealthy Mexicans up from Monterrey, Nuevo Laredo alien smugglers, Las Vegas chatterboxes, and a smattering of California professional suntans. Yeah, it struck me as ultra-Texan. Christ, I thought, if Santa Anna's critics ever saw this scene, they would forgive the Alamo.

Heck, they might ask him to do it again.

A short, fat Mexican woman in a white dress came by with a silver tray of manhattans and tequila sunrises. Elaine took the tequila and I took one of each. Yes, I said to myself, Ace could get used to this real fast. I thought about the lumber mill in Oregon and the spot welding job I'd lost in Lansing and just shook my head. Crap, man, I thought, I guess it takes a lot of us posthole diggers to keep the rich in ranches or a lot of folks pumping gas into their cars or a lot of junkies pumping shit into their veins. Yeah, I thought about the airplane I'd seen a couple of evenings back. Wherever it'd been going—well, I didn't want to know where it was going.

I killed both of the drinks and leaned against the white

fence rail, just upwind from the Chanel fumes of four or
five old ladies, each looking as if she had just stepped out
of fourteen hours' worth of beauty shop construction and
pancake baking. They smoked cigarettes through long
holders and wore a short ton of makeup. The cigarette
smoke came out of their mouths in long sentences of nico-
tine exhaust.

Elaine tapped me on the shoulder and I followed her.
We walked over to the first horse barn and moseyed beneath the gingerbread lathework of the open stable door. I
felt the soft slap of air-conditioned air. "I guess you need
cool air for million-dollar horses," Elaine remarked ab-
sently. An astroturf strip ran down the middle of the stable hall. We walked on top of it toward the rear of the
half-lit building. I smelled the sickeningly sweet scent of
mint-fresh muck. Two jockeys stood by the last stall
smoking a joint. They offered us a hit and I refused. Elaine
thought about it, then said no thanks.

We left through the rear door. A wide green field sloped
to the north, leveled off, and became a long sod runway. A
half dozen or so Beeches and Cessnas were parked along
the smooth bermuda strip, an orange wind sock was
hanging slack from its pole. In the distance a low whine
became a tree-hopping four-seat Cessna. The plane set-
tled and landed, kicking up a cloud of dust and cut grass.
It taxied down the runway and stopped. A man and a
woman got out, stretched, then proceeded to unload case
after case of scotch into the golf cart that zipped across
the field to meet them.

"Damn," I said. Elaine didn't seem to notice. She had
her compact out and was staring at the mirror. She shut
the powder box with a soft click.

We walked around the long stable, passing a bright-
blue dining fly that covered a group of angry, shouting
voices crowding around a sawdust pit. I checked it out.

The anger turned to happiness as two slim fighting cocks began to stab each other with sharpened spurs. One dying bird spit a thin stream of blood onto the yellow blouse of a blond matron wearing eyeglasses with rhinestone rims.

"My God," Elaine said, matter-of-factly.

"That outta be illegal," I said.

"It is," she replied. "But then lots of things are illegal."

"Between consenting adults?" I asked.

"Wouldn't know," she fired back, "I'm always fending off children."

I decided to shut my mouth and this time keep it tight.

We sidled up to the white track rail and watched a couple of short cowboys, yeah, short cowboys, exercise their quarter horses. Elaine leaned over and almost bit my ear, before she whispered "I'm going up to the house to see some friends."

I liked her breath in my ear and told her so. She jabbed me in the ribs. "Why don't you stay here, Bill, and see if you can pick up a tip on a hot horse."

"You mean, on which one is drugged and which one isn't?"

Another golf cart with mixed drinks came by, and Elaine put an icy gin and tonic in my hand. "Enjoy the atmosphere," she said. More alcohol, I thought, looking at the drink and sniffing it. Heck, it wasn't even eleven o'clock.

I watched Elaine's sculpted ass rotate toward the mansion, took another sip from my drink, then wandered along the rail, checking out the women and the horses. The liquor was already in my spine and I felt half-grooved, up near the top so to speak.

Then I stepped on a cocker spaniel and the poor dog yelped like I'd tried to run it down with a bulldozer. "Gee, I'm sorry," I said to the old woman who started to yell and scream like she was the animal that I'd stepped on. She called me a stupid oaf. "Hell, I'm drunk, lady," I said, hunkering down to pat the pup behind the ears. "He's an affectionate little feller, isn't he, ma'am?" I steadied myself, shoulder against white fence slat. The old woman took the dog and gave it a kiss, and except for my spilled gin and tonic the world was almost realigned and I was six feet or so closer to sobriety.

Which, in retrospect, was a dose of good luck.

"Don't know Paco."

A flat, cold voice.

"And he steps on stray dogs even 'fore they shit."

Whoa. Rocking on my heels, I rose. I rose slow like and turned around. Blaine stood alone at the rail, watching me, his optics now like a pair of gray dice come up snake eyes.

"Why, howdy, Blaine."

The big man stiffened his lips. "Had a little ack-see-dent with the dawg, huh, Billy? Is it still Billy?" I nodded. Blaine gripped the track rail so tight that his knuckles were white. His entire body seemed like it was being pulled taut, set to explode. "So," he said slowly, "I heard you went and got yourself a job . . . workin' for Paco. You like your job?"

"Yeah. Pay's pretty good. While it lasts."

Blaine arched one of his nonexistent eyebrows as his sun-cured face and forehead wrinkled into a plain of angry thought. He reached into his shirt pocket, pulled out a yellow jellybean, and popped the candy into his unhinged jaw. "What they got you *doin'*, 'sides fixing fence and digging shit holes?" he asked, sucking on the drop.

I almost, not quite but almost, got the impression that Blaine was trying to be subtle, mostly because he acted as if he were more interested in confronting the sky than confronting me.

"Gee, nothin' much. Oh, they ask me to stomp out a dog every now and then."

Blaine moved his shoulders around like he was trying to shake a knot out of his head, then he spit hard on the ground, the jelly bean flying out like a bullet. "How come you're a candyass liar?" he said. I didn't like his question and I told him so. He just shook his head and spit again, "Course you're a liar, 'bout you and Paco, ain't you? I asked you," he said, sticking his thumb in his chest, "I asked you last week how long you knowed him and you try and come on like you're some dumbshit ho-bo." He cocked his head. "Don't you go bullshitting me no more, y'heah, Billy boy, or you're gonna get snakebit. And that is dumbshit." He looked at me, waiting for me to do something. I didn't move. I think I grinned a dumbshit hobo's grin.

But Blaine must have thought I was being chickenshit. He got stupid. He grabbed the collar of my shirt and gave it a tight grip. "Now, mistah, tell me, tell me how you know Paco—Mistah Frank Ramirez. And where's it from, Houston?"

Blaine shouldn't have touched me. I slapped his hand off my collar and pushed the dude back against the rail, my forearm under his chin. We're gonna fight, I thought, and this goat-roper might beat the hell out of me. But I couldn't take his poking, I can't take that kind of poking, not if I got the breath to poke back.

Held against the rail, Blaine relaxed. Four or five folks started looking at us. Blaine dropped his hands. I let him go and he grinned. "So you're a nasty-ass," he said, then spit.

"I didn't lie to anybody," I said. Well, he wasn't going to try anything, at least not now. There was a streak of the calculator in Blaine—otherwise, he'd have never made it to early middle age. "What's got you all wound around the nerves, Blaine? Why do you even give a damn?"

He coughed and popped another jelly bean in his mouth. "There's somethin' about you that's all wrong.

Real wrong. I ain't figured it through yet, but I'm working on it. Your shit smells, Billy bad-ass."

"Uh, why don't you, uh . . . go fuck a goat, Blaine, you know, put your dong in a sewer."

The line didn't faze him. He pointed his finger gunlike at my chest as he leaned back against the rail post. "You musta knowed Paco from way back, the way I read it. School . . . or somewhere."

I folded my arms. "Now let's you and me get a couple of basics down. First off, why's it matter?"

Blaine rapped the fence with his knuckles. "Matter? Now you're going dumbshit again. And I don't buy the dumbshit. You both move around like a couple of smart boys. I don't like smart boys. I don't like the way they look. You get them funny college ideas."

"College? Shit. I went to Wayne State for three semesters and flunked out."

"Wherezat."

"Wayne State. De-troit. Christ, Blaine, I'm an all-American dumbshit, just like you."

Blaine blinked. He was carefully unrelaxing. He took a mechanical aim. Bang. He hit the rail post with his fist. No vibration. He opened his palm. "See, Billy-boy, I think you're a buddy of Paco's out of Houston. Or is it Washington, D.C.?"

"Huh?" That threw me. I waved him off. "Man, you got some fucked-up ideas." Yeah, that really threw me. I tried to put his psychotic cowboy crap into some kind of single notion. What fits. I shook my head. "What's got you so stinking mad? You a lunatic? You got a hard-on 'cause a Mex is hanging out with a rich white chick?"

Blaine blinked again, slow like. Then he laughed, dropped his jaw, and laughed some more. "With that—that Masterson bitch? Hey, is Paco pumpin' her? Or maybe she's pumpin' him?" He tossed his head back, leaning back and looking at the cloudless sky. "Boy, I think you really are some dumbshit. Pure dog dumbshit. Oh yeah, that's it man, that's why I'm so, uh, so stinking mad. Hey, Billy bad-ass, you must have one good brain." Blaine turned around to face the track as five quarter horses blew past, then he faced me and laughed again. "So, ole Paco's pumpin' that bitch." He pulled a pack of Camels out of his front pocket and lit a cigarette. A Mexican lady with a tray full of drinks came by, and I plucked off a shot glass of straight Irish whiskey and drained it.

Blaine took a long time-buying drag on the cigarette. "So you gonna watch out for your own ass from now on, huh, Billy bad-ass?" I just looked at him. He blew a ring of smoke into the air and started laughing again, the wrinkles in his rock-hard face cracking into shallow fault lines. "He's balling her. Yeah, that's it man, you must know exactly why I'm mad. She-it," he snickered. "That's the very reason." Blaine took another drag on his Camel, then paused. "Tell you what, Billy boy. We need some fence work on the Dickson side of the line. Hell, we can always use a big guy like you. Work for me and I'll pay you, what, $220 a week? Why, I'll give you twice what tight-ass Masterson's paying you. That's super pay for, a what, a hitchhiker?" He broadened his sneer into a passable grin.

"Hey, Blaine, good buddy," I said, tapping him hard on one of his pearl buttons, "You don't know something about me that you of all folks need to know."

His face narrowed. "What's that?"

"I don't work for loudmouth cocksuckers."

He hadn't expected that, but then I hadn't either— maybe the Irish whiskey brought it on. Maybe it was more fun watching Blaine go cowboy psycho. His eyes had just about popped back into his skull when he found the voice to snarl, "I warned you, Billy bad-ass. You got your shot. Now you're in for some deep shit." He threw his cigarette out on the track and took a hike toward the stables.

Round one to Buchanan. No, maybe this was round two

'cause I'd sassed ole Blaine in the gas station. I watched him leave. He wasn't gonna look back, not today. But the hell he cares about Elaine and Paco hitting the sack, not that they were really balling 'cause I didn't know. What did I know? I know. I knew ole cowboy Blaine was five-eighths wacko. I knew he'd three-eighths tried to muscle me, for no first-class reason. But then we'd both been drinking and God knows liquored cowboys in the sun either fall asleep or start fighting. Ok—Blaine and Ramirez had an angry thing. Let them pound it out. I'd move on, get some distance. Get some more whiskey. But I didn't need any more whiskey. The damn psycho just shouldn't have put his hands on me. But why should I get into a bother, I thought, looking at the empty shot glass. Blaine and I were about the same size, I might even be a little heftier. In a straight-on, clean fight, I might just take him. But Blaine, no use fooling myself, Blaine was a bushwhack kind of guy, a man with a blackjack waiting in the alley. I'd watch my ass all right, but if we got down, I didn't plan on losing. Billy Bad-ass. Yeah, I liked the image, Billy Bad-ass Buchanan. It dawned on me that maybe I'd scored a few points with Paco just by being good-size and a combat vet. Trouble on the ranch, yeah, I could handle that cowboy idea—iffn I wasn't too shit-faced drunk.

My forehead was lying on top of the fence post. I jerked my head up. Blaine had disappeared. Pop—their smoke from the starter's pistol.

I'm gonna have to slow this drinking down, I said to myself as I looked down the track rail. Four quarter horses, which to my half-corked head added up to one full horse, were tearing down the sod track, whipping past with a blur of jockey colors and the smell of horse and earth.

"Damn," I muttered. "That's pretty."

"Yeah. And that's fifteen hunnert bucks." The guy standing just down the rail, nodding a soupy sort of nod, hoisted a martini glass like a Roman salute to the sun.

"You musta won, I guess."

"Yeah." He finished off the martini and signaled one of the waiters. "N'other," he said.

He looked to be about six feet tall, brown hair and brown eyes, maybe a man of twenty-eight stuck with a forty-five-year-old nose, in terms of the dull ruddy pits asssociated with active alcoholism. His blue knit golf shirt sported a JD monogram. The uncuffed white double pants topped a pair of white tie shoes.

"You gotta be some asshole from Dallas," I said.

He burped. The Mexican lady with the tray came by and he hooked a tall double martini. I got another shot glass of straight Irish, this time with a cube. "My name's Jarret Davis," he said, cocking an eye. "Didn't you used to play for the Oilers?"

I had to think a second. The last time I'd played a down of football was freshman year in high school. I'd made all my muscles pushing grocery carts and baling hay. Hmmm. I took a slow sip of whiskey and looked into Jarret's bloodshot eyes.

"Yeah," he continued, "I'm sure you did. Linebacker, wasn't it?" I swished the Irish around and nodded a sort of yeah. "Well no lie," Jarret said, "I saw you turn on that cowboy." He raised his forearm, miming what I'd done to Blaine. "That's what you boys do on pass defense, isn't it? Put an elbow up." He burped again. "I was sure I recognized you. Lemme see now, you're ... you're ..."

"Bill Bad-ass," I said.

"Bill Baddus? Why sure. You used to play second string behind, uh," he began to snap his fingers as if the noise would supply the missing name. I couldn't help him, 'specially since I was lying. Anyway I couldn't think of anybody who ever played for the Oilers, at least since they traded Earl Campbell. "Uh, you played behind . . . Brazile, right? Behind Bob Brazile." I gave another sort of yeah. Jarret grinned. "Yep, if there's anything I know, it's football, least ways Texas football." He drained the tall martini and flung the glass over his shoulder. It hit a pin oak and shattered.

"Hey, Davis. You come here often?"

He nodded and burped. "Four or five times a year. Your first ex-cur-shun?" I nodded. "You having a good time?" he asked.

"I like the free booze," I replied. I pointed toward the house. "This whole joint looks on the high side of expensive."

"Yep," Jarret agreed with a wink, "trite but true. But when you got it, you got it, or in ole Dolf's case, you inherited from a Daddy that stole it . . . then you stole some more." Davis lit a filter cigarette, inhaled, then let the smoke blow from his reddened nostrils. "Well, tell me all about the life of an ex-pro football player."

I shrugged. "You got to hustle to survive."

"Bet you still get the chicks."

I pointed my thumb toward the ground. "It's a downhill slide once you leave the sports pages."

Jarret shook his head. "I could have figured as much," he said, tossing his cigarette to the turf and stomping it out.

Another horse race began and ended, won by a chestnut quarter horse filly. "How'd you do?" I asked.

He winced and pulled out a toothpick. "Think I won. Couple of grand." A loudspeaker announced the results, then crackled and became an ear-splitting buzz. The announcer stopped the screech and came back on and apologized.

"Where you from originally, Bill?" Jarret asked.

I told him something. "What about yourself?"

"Houston. You gotta know River Oaks." He raised an eyebrow. I didn't know nothin', but I nodded like everything was understood to be the obvious. "Shit," he volunteered, "I went to Lamar, even tried to play a little football. You know about Lamar?" he asked. I nodded like everything was understood. "I bet you do," he said. "Yep. Tried to go to U of H and quit. Screwed around a lot. Spoiled rich kid life-style, y'know."

"Don't think I do know," I said.

Jarret pulled a toothpick out of his shirt pocket and began to try to rub a headache off his forehead.

"What's this Dolf Dickson guy look like? D'you know?" I asked.

He pulled a small metal case out of his hip pocket and popped a button. The case separated, revealing the stereo lense of a small field glass. He pointed the glasses across the track. "He's the dude in the red western blazer, standing next to the fat New York wop." I took the glasses and found the blazer—gray-haired man enclosed—then homed in on a halter top tight-on-the breasts I recognized as Azure's. About a dozen people down the rail from Dolf I found Elaine. She had her gold compact out and she was just snapping it shut. Seemed like she aimed that compact, I thought. Hmmm. Well, Billy ain't all that stupid.

"So tell me a little about Dolf Dickson," I said.

"It's all true, everything," Jarret replied, "about LBJ and Dickson's old man I mean. Price Dickson and Lyndon were just like that, like two fingers as tight as a doctor's snakes," he continued, crossing his index and middle fingers.

"What's Johnson have to do with all this?"

Jarret shushed me and we watched the last leg of another race. "Damn. There goes four grand," he said, setting his field glasses back down on the rail. "Hey, you mean you don't know about the Dicksons of Duval County and LBJ? What kind of Texan are you?"

"One that's most recently from Michigan," I said.

Jarret snickered. "Yeah, there're a lot more of you creeps down here all the time. But I don't mean nothing by that," he said, raising his palm, "I mean, you came down here with a legitimate job, playing football and all."

The golf cart with drinks came by and we each took two. "So how come you know so much about this political corruption?" I asked.

"Well, uh, my old man used to work for 'em . . . for all of 'em. Lyndon, Price Dickson, Dolf."

"What'd he do?"

"What all lawyers do. Fix their taxes. Kiss their asses. Yeah, my old man used to be some kind of tax lawyer. Top flight."

"Used to be?"

Jarret smiled a slick smile. "Shit. Can't stay in the Bar Association if you're in jail. Even the Texas Bar Association."

"Yeah. Guess you can't."

"Well, he isn't in jail anymore, so don't pour out the old can of sympathy. In fact," Jarret said, picking up the field glasses and siting them on a distant rim of the rail, "that big ole cowboy in the blue denim suit's my old man. Have a look."

I had a look. I saw a set of heavy jowls and a sagging face staring into the bottom of a highball. "What's he do these days?" I asked.

"Drinks . . . wishes he was dead," Jarret replied, kicking back a slug of what I figured was straight Jim Beam. "Thinks about box 13."

Something in my sot flesh brain clicked. "Now I've heard of that—box 13 in Duval County, the one where the dead folks voted for Johnson. Is that story for real?"

"So you know about that one, huh. Well pawd-nuh, it was box 13 in Jim Wells County first off, but you got the bottom line down. Yeah, the dead voted, thanks to this old Dickson housekeeper, uh, Miz Thomasson. She's the one that used all the red ink."

"What's that mean?"

"Gee, thought you knew the basic stuff. You know about voter registration rolls?" I said I thought I did. "Well, all the folks at number 13 polling place, even the dead ones, they just happened to write down their names in the same red ink and in the same handwriting." Jarret grinned a backwards grin. "Am I communicating?"

"Yeah. So the votes were faked. But how come somebody didn't ask for a recount?"

"Of the ballots? Come on, you think a shark like Price Dickson stays on top by being slow? The ballots got burned, accidental like you understand, so that Dickson can testify on the stand that he didn't do nothin' with them. There's this old hoot by the name of Wershmeier, lived down near Dickson's other ranch. He's got a couple more of these babies y'know," Jarret said, moving his hand. "A super one up by Corsicana. Anyway Wershmeier and his wife live down by the Dickson spread that's south of Freer. Well, Miz Wershmeier was your typical dingbat housewife—dizzy, impulsive, a gossip, that's her reputation, right? Ole Price calls her up and says hey honey, we're gonna have a barbecue, could you cook some of those tasty little Kraut sausages? She comes toddling over and Price and her husband get to drinking, then Price says he plumb forgot to start the fire. Seein' as he and Wershmeier are talking business, would the lady mind? There's some paper and kindling in the kitchen. Why sure, she says, she doesn't mind. She takes the voter rolls off the kitchen table. When the feds show up Price gives 'em all a link of barbecued sausage and Lyndon wins by eighty-seven votes. Price says he doesn't know what happened to those votes and Miz Wershmeier doesn't know shit."

I snorted and almost spilled my drink. "Seems the cops could have cracked that in a flash. Naw," I concluded, thinking a minute, "the local cops would have been owned."

"Right in Dickson's back pocket," Jarret added.

"Standard situation," I muttered. "But what about Lyndon's opponent? He must have been pissing blood."

"Coke Stevenson? Get real. Old Coke used to run the same scam up in East Texas, 'specially when he was governor. Even the dead-vote Coke, 'cause he's the real thing." Jarret laughed. "Lyndon had so much dirt on Coke that 'cept for a few feds and Harry Truman there'd never have been an investigation."

I said that I was flat ass-tounded.

"Hey, buddy, that's politics. Get out of your helmet and look around." Jarret went on talking, about Coke Stevenson and somebody named Ma Ferguson.

I picked up the field glasses, focused them, and found the chick with the white halter top. "That woman. What's her name. Azure?"

"Don't touch that bitch. She's got Dickson branded on her bikini. I mean it."

"Hey. I sort of like challenges."

"You might not like being dead."

My back developed a vein of ice. I liked being alive. As things stood, I could leave her and everything else alone. I bit my lip and checked once more. She was beautiful, in that breezy, blonde way of being beautiful.

"You growing horns?" Jarret asked. He snickered again. "Hey, buddy. Now if you really want to check out a class piece, ah, just come on."

He started motioning with his finger, but stopped as another race finished. Jarret smiled and said he'd just won three grand and that would be his betting day. We walked down the rail, picked up another round of drinks—I'd stopped counting—then headed for the white mansion, toward a small group of people sitting in chaise longues around the white stone swimming pool.

"Now," Jarret said, stumbling, his hand giving an alcoholic wave, "you talk about a classy little case of easy. She's so—hey, Anne, I've got someone I want you to meet."

A short brunette sat in an aluminum folding chair, nursing a mixed drink. She wasn't dressed for swimming—she wore a pair of brown capri pants and a black pullover.

She didn't look up at Jarret.

"Hey, Annie, I want you to meet my friend, uh, Billy. This is my buddy Billy. You'll like him, I mean, he's a real jock y'know. Billy, this here in the chair's Anne. You all say hello."

"Fuck off, Jarret," Anne said to her mixed drink.

Jarret laughed a horse's laugh, and I guess that was the moment I completely realized we were both drunk as skunks. "Why little honey," he said slowly, "whyn you talk that way to old Jarret? You must think I'm ugly or something . . ."

Anne looked at me. "Listen, I don't know who you are, but you're really bringing yourself down to hang around with this kind of scum."

"The name's Bill," I replied, extending my hand.

"You're both stinking drunk." Anne became exasperated. She set her drink down and stood up.

"Whatsa matter, Annie hunny? Doan like old Jarret no more?" He tried to put his arms around her waist but she pushed him away with a sharp slap. Jarret raised his fist to strike her.

The next thing I saw was Jarret landing in the pool, tossed there by a man about my size. Jarret came up coughing out chlorinated water.

I went after the man who'd thrown him. The dude had a long wax mustache and a swarthy complexion, like a fast-class Arab, I thought, just before he executed a second perfect judo throw and I flew backassward into the pool.

When I crawled out, Jarret and Anne were spewing marital obscenities at each other and the Arab bodyguard was doing his best to separate them. His black-brown eyes focused on me, just as I felt a long streak of mean igniting. The bodyguard stepped back, and Anne and Jarret fell out of the way as I rushed Mr. Judo.

Just fuck his black belt, I thought.

He tried to come up with some kind of body cross and feint. I blocked his leg kick with my forearm and put a fist out for his jaw, only he ducked, the poor dumb sumbitch. He tried to go down under the blow and my strike put knuckles into his temple. Lights out.

I watched him collapse, then felt a little wobbly in my own knees. The quick sucker'd put a flat hand punch into my chest so fast I'd barely been aware of the motion. But my body was aware of the blow. I bent over like I was going to throw up a week's worth of cookies. Wait a sec. I put my hand on my stomach, took a deep breath, then shook off the wave of nausea.

Jarret was stomping away, after telling Anne one last time just where she could put her head. I followed him over to an astroturf putting green, where we both collapsed.

"Okay," I finally said, "what's the story here?"

He took off his JD monogrammed golf shirt and winced. "You just met my ex-wife."

"You were going to set me up with your wife?"

"Ex-wife. X!" He traced the letter in the air. "Christ, I was so drunk I didn't know what I was doing." He almost sobbed, then decided to spit instead.

"I see why she's your ex. You talk to her like shit."

Jarret turned red, then rubbed his eyeballs. "Everybody talks to their ex like that. It wasn't always so spicy."

"I dunno. I wouldn't talk to a dog that way," I said.

"I was drunk," Jarret insisted.

"Yeah. You were something." I lay back on the astroturf and watched the putting green's pen flag wave weakly in the almost breeze. "You sure took a swan dive," I said with a smile.

Jarret agreed. "Didn't plan on the bodyguard. All I wanted to do was talk a little, but that woman never has time to say nothing."

"Hey. Who was that masked man?"

"Some hired gigolo—naw, some guy her old man hired to keep me away from his *pristine* daughter. He's some Neofascist Turk's all I know." Jarret Davis was beginning to sulk. "S'all spoiled rotten, y'know. Look, I'm sorry, real sorry." He stood up. "See you later, huh?"

"Yeah. Later." I rolled over and groaned. "A lot later."

He started walking in a half-aimed way toward the pecan grove and the line of Caddies and Mercedes-Benzes. I rested a couple of minutes, got up from the green and put some saliva on my fingers, rubbing it on my face. The chlorine was already starting to dry around my eyes and ears, and the chemical itched.

Then I looked back toward the pool. Somebody had fished my black Resistol out of the water, and Anne was taking it from him. Her bodyguard sat on a chaise longue, holding what looked to be an ice pack against his head. She tossed my hat on a patio table and sat back in her chair.

I walked over to the pool. She was nursing a new drink

when I arrived. "Peace brother," I said, giving the V-sign to her bodyguard.

He grinned, but Anne gave me a fierce slice of a look. "What do you want?" she demanded.

"To apologize. I want to apologize," I said as I sat down beside her, "and to get my hat. I'm real sorry lady. We were pretty drunk, but that's no real excuse."

"You a friend of Jarret's?" she asked.

I shook my head. "Not really. Just met him."

Anne was without a doubt quite beautiful and much younger than I'd first imagined. I'd thought she was forty-five—it was more like the late twenties.

"Well, all right then," she said, "I accept. That's very nice of you."

The bodyguard took a sip out of a Perrier bottle. "Nice punch," he remarked.

"Thanks," I replied.

"I was more impressed with the forearm block. Real strong, and quick too. That leg kick usually kills," he said matter-of-factly. I didn't say anything. "Where'd you learn to do that?" he asked.

"See that?" I asked him as I curled my arm and popped out a bicep. "It comes from digging postholes. I didn't pay some squint-eyed Zen master to put'em on me."

The Arab, who I decided looked more like a Turk—it was something about the cut of the brow—just looked amused. "Ah so," he said. "Domo."

"Rudi used to work in Europe, was it Istanbul? That's where you learned all those nasty things, isn't it, Rudi?"

He shook his head for a no. "Italian security school," he said.

"Rudi, why don't you get Mr. . . . ."

"Buchanan. Bill Buchanan."

"Mr. Buck-cannon something cool," Anne finished.

"Something nonalcoholic I hope?" Rudi asked sarcastically.

"Yeah. A shot of soda'll do fine."

I turned back toward Anne. She was giving my body the old head to toe treatment. She smiled. "I don't know what Jarret told you, Bill, but I'm not such a bitch. I'm not a nympho either."

"I believe you. He really didn't say much of anything. He strikes me as a kind of half-zonked."

"How about half-psychotic? Can't blame him completely though." She took a sip of her drink, then set it down and pulled her sweater off, revealing a nice tanned torso and a bikini top, breasts not too chesty but firm and nice. "Why waste the sun," she said.

"Yeah. Seems like you've got enough of it around here to waste." She asked me where I came from and I told her, then she said she was from Houston originally but had moved to Corpus Christi. She said she thought she knew half of the people at the track, always the same buzzards in her flock. Her voice sounded light and pleasant.,

Rudi arrived with the soda and ice, and I started to drain it but stopped as a hand—a sensual woman's hand—touched the small of my back and then ran up to my shoulders.

"Ulp," I said.

It was Elaine, sunglasses firmly glued to the bridge of her nose. "If I'd known you wanted to swim, we could have brought a suit. You ought to take that shirt off."

"Pants too," Anne said with a wink.

"We gotta go, boss lady?" I asked.

Elaine nodded. "Head'em up."

"Uh, are you sober?" I asked Elaine.

She held her palm out flat and it didn't even quiver. "Like a stone." She paused. "How have you been, Anne Raymond?" Elaine asked.

Anne and Elaine batted around a couple of pleasantries and commented on the Davises' finalized divorce. I got the distinct impression they'd known each other a long time.

"So, Mr. Buchanan is working for you, Elaine?" Anne asked with a suggestive twist of the grammar.

"Yes. For my foreman."

"You know Paco Ramirez?" I asked Anne.

"Paco Ramirez?" She shook her head and said no. "I haven't been to the Masterson place in years." Elaine and I started to leave. "Well, Bill, I hope, uh . . ." Anne began.

"That we run into each other sometime," I said.

Anne nodded.

"Great getting to know you," Rudi said, dropping the ice pack from his temple to reveal a nice blue bump.

"I hope you continue to think so," I said. "You shouldn't have hit me. I didn't do nothin' to you."

"You were in the area of violence," he replied. "And you don't look like a peacenik."

Elaine and Anne said good-bye, and I followed Miz Masterson across the backyard and through the grove.

We reached the car. "Oh Christ," Elaine said as she was opening the door. She looked sort of sheepish.

"Forget something?"

"Not really," she said, slipping into the car and dropping her purse by the gear shift. "No . . . oh hell, just wait a second." She got out of the car and started walking toward the ranch house.

"Where you going?" I yelled after her.

"To the john. Is that all right with you?"

Well, I couldn't follow her there, so I watched her stomp across the long front lawn, taking the most direct route to the house. Shoot, I thought, women really do have a plumbing problem. A man can just find a convenient tree.

Then I saw her purse and the brain clicked and curiosity got the better of my fingers. But not before I pulled a wad of Kleenex out of the glove compartment and used it to keep my fingerprints to myself.

The gold compact was right near the top. I popped the latch and it opened and, yeah, at the end of the powder case a little rectangular slide opened to reveal the glass lense. Kodak must have been conspiring with Revlon to produce this gadget.

I snapped the camera shut and put it back in the purse. Five or six minutes later Elaine returned to the car, her general demeanor unimproved. She didn't suspect a thing. "Strap your seat belt on, slugger," she said.

" 'Nother wild ride?" I asked.

She just grinned.

Elaine didn't take the short route home. She said she wanted to show me some country, and I took that as a possible come-on, a verbal reflection of the sensual hand up the spine, but her ice-cool voice and the rich-bitch attitude squashed that idea. Yeah, she meant what she said, I guess, and not an iota more or less, though to my way of thinking she was the only terrain worth seeing. So I sat there, riding shotgun in her Mercedes, saying my yesma'ams and watching weeds and cactus while Elaine cut between Sunday drivers and zipped around express buses going to Laredo.

I wasn't going to ask her about the camera. At least not yet.

It was mid-afternoon when we reached Chorillo, and we went into La Fiesta and had a couple of enchiladas and tamales. We got back to the ranch well before sunset.

"Keep the black hat, Bill," she said as we stopped in her driveway, "it looks good on you."

I walked back to the bunkhouse, feeling happy, sad, cheated, and a little on the good side of nice.

**7**

PACO WOKE ME UP early. "It's Monday. You still want to work?"

I yawned and rubbed my eyes. "I didn't come into this world to be an unemployment statistic. 'Course I do."

"Well, that's good to hear. I thought you might have decided you'd be better off racing horses or something."

"I'm not that crooked." Paco walked out of the room and down the hall. "Hey, Pock, what time did you crawl in last night?"

"Too late," he called from the living room.

By the time I got in the kitchen Paco was already dealing out two plates of eggs. "I heard you almost broke a Turk cop's jaw."

"Say whaa?" I asked. "I thought I hit a bodyguard."

Paco shrugged. "Bodyguard, cop, whatever." He poured himself a second cup of coffee. "You must have hit him square." I nodded and said yeah. "Well," Paco sneered, "I figured you for someone who wouldn't pull a punch. You're not afraid to mix it, are you, Billy?"

I took another bite of egg and swallowed. "The truth is, I'm completely chickenshit. I don't fight that much and I don't talk half as tough as other cowards do. But if I'm gonna do it, somethin's not going to be getting up."

Paco let out a wry laugh. "You and me both," he said. "But when you're dealing with Blaine Rawlins, you watch your ass. He's a case and a half." He paused. "I'll take care of Blaine," he said, rising from the table.

Paco went back to his room, and I popped a couple of vitamin tabs in my mouth. So Paco was well informed. I guess Elaine had seen me arguing with Blaine. Hadn't I punched that sucker in the chest? Or was it the chin? And I had hit that Turk, that Turk bodyguard. Or was it cop? Maybe Miz Masterson had the film on file. If Blaine and I ever went a couple of rounds, maybe her little gold compact could supply *Sports Illustrated* with a set of color prints.

Paco and I washed the dishes and then split.

I noticed that somebody'd already put a whole load of new siding in the back of the pickup. And I said so. "Hey, man, it's okay, I confess," Paco said. "You don't have to sound like you're giving me the third degree, huh?" We left and I was driving.

Paco told me to stop off at the first corral. "Stay in the truck. I just wanta drop off a couple of things," he said. I leaned against the door, listening to the farm report on WOAI San Antonio. In the rearview mirror I could see Paco haul a piece of aluminum siding out of the truck. He dropped the siding just out of view, then came back to the rear of the truck and started tugging on a long roll of green tarp. I turned away from the mirror and looked across the draw, to where it broadened into a little valley. A pair of crows sat in a dead tree, preening themselves. They both spotted something moving in the weeds, watched it, then, like a pair of raven warplanes, dived to the ground. There was a silent flutter—whatever they saw, they hit.

Paco got back in the cab. "I dumped some new stuff back over there in the brush," he said, pointing in a vague direction, "behind the corral. Just so you know, okay?"

Still leaning against the door, I gave him the thumbs-up sign and started the engine. "Hey," I asked him lazily, "when'd you get all that new siding?"

Paco stared at the road, either ignoring my question or looking for the ridgeline. "Came in yesterday. Why do you ask?"

I tipped back my gimme hat. "Just curious. You didn't say anything about a load of stuff coming in on Sunday . . ."

"Didn't I?" he said, glancing at me and then back at the road. He shrugged. "So what?"

"We get anything else?"

"An aluminum gate, some wiring. Nothing special."

I made a tricky turn, swung the wheel around, and turned the truck onto the ridge track. "Where we going to use the gate?"

"Hey, it's already used. I put it in yesterday, up at the baby corral on the southwest side. Guess you're glad that's finished, huh? You really sunk some holes in that rocky bitch."

I sort of sat up. "Why'd you go and do it yourself? I'd have helped you. I didn't particularly want to go horse racing."

"Heck, I got bored. Slow Sunday, nobody home."

"I thought you didn't like working on Sunday."

He shot a cutting glance at me, the cold flare of calculation in his brown eyes. "It wasn't any problem, Bill. And that's no bullshit."

I believed him. Christ, he was easy to believe. Besides, I liked to work on my lonesome, just me and my muscles and the sun and nobody around to yell at you, so why shouldn't Paco get off on that scene? Fine. Some truck delivers building materials on Sunday, while I'm gone, while I'm hustled off, what's in that, right? I bit my lip and thought about the powder puff camera and Blaine and the airplane and I decided to just sit on it. 'Til later, I thought, 'til this evening—then I'm going to get some straight talk from Paco, with no ifs ands or buts.

So we didn't say anything more until we reached the ridge. We got out and I stuck my carbine on top of a pile of fence posts. "I bought myself a new shotgun, Bill," Paco said. He pulled a beautiful Browning automatic out of a rifle case that lay next to the truck's built-in toolbox. "You like it?"

"Yeah. Is it a 12-gauge?" He nodded. "When'd you get it?"

"Last week. In San Antonio."

I looked at him for a long second. "How come you're just now getting around to showing it to me?"

Paco surprised me. "Billy boy, what's all this hostility and suspicion? You're showing signs of latent paranoia heading toward expressive schizophrenia."

"I got a case of active paranoia. And you talk like you took some kind of freshman psychology class."

"Took more than that," Paco replied with a lilt. "B.S. in electrical engineering, University of Houston. M.S. at Cal Tech. I really moved on the GI Bill."

I gave a low awed whistle. "Heavy credentials. What're you doing down on the farm?"

"I like the farm," he said sarcastically.

"Man, with all those degrees seems to me somebody'd have gone and snapped you up for a big-bucks job."

Paco put his new shotgun back in its case and zipped it shut. "Who says somebody hasn't?" he asked, sticking his tongue in his cheek.

I put my boot on the truck's back bumper and looked at him. "I'm afraid I don't understand."

"Save it for later," Paco replied in a voice that said to cool it. "I'm going up the ridge." He put the shotgun case back down in the truck bed.

"It's pretty near finished up there," I said.

"I know." He opened the toolbox and pulled out a roll of electric tape, put a pair of needle-nosed pliers in his pocket, then picked up a short strand of wire and a retractable tape measure. "Why don't you start picking up some of the loose pieces around here, like throwing that tarp and those extra posts in the truck? I'll be back in a minute."

I said okay and got to it. Paco started up the ridge to the crest, and I started rolling up a long loop of wire.

In South Texas on a summer's day noon begins a little after eight in the morning. Like, it's hot. Already sweating, I loaded up the loose wire and the tarps, started collecting scattered fence posts, put a dozen or so posts in the truck, then went to the watercooler for a drink.

Fifteen minutes, a half hour?

That's when I heard the rifle shot. One shot, clean, clear, sharp as anger and a bolt of fear.

I grabbed my carbine and scrambled up the path, kicking stone and dust, losing my hat on a scrub tree limb, slicing hell out of my jeans on a nest of thorn and prickly pear. I couldn't hear anything except my own gut breathing and the whip of mesquite leaves and the soft crash of cowboy boots on heat-cracked earth.

Then came the hard breath of heat and the hardest silence.

Paco lay between two empty postholes, a 30-caliber-looking bullet hole in his chest. I held his head. His back, where the bullet emerged, was a sluggish mass of red and brown and bits of shirt and bone. I looked across the vista, the wide stretch of cactus and scrub mesquite that opened toward the Dickson Ranch.

Nothing moved, not even the leaves in the not-so-distant tree line of twisted oak and deadwood.

# 8

THEY LET ME out of the hoosegow three days later. Actually the San Diego, Texas, jail was halfway decent, as jails go. They at least fed you something besides vitamin-enriched swill. One of the deputies—a fat Mex named Fraydo—even let me take a shower in the cops' bathroom because the plumbing in the inmate facilities was being repaired. He waited outside the shower curtain, playing with a Rubik's cube, a .44 Magnum slung in his shoulder holster. As I showered, I sang Beatles tunes and whistled "Dixie."

Yeah, they arrested me for shooting Paco, and I didn't see or hear nothin' about my rights or about an attorney or any of that ACLU stuff. Not that the cops were so tough. They barely interrogated me.

And I thought I'd been such a perfect Boy Scout. I carried Paco down across my shoulders and set him on a tarp in the back of the truck. He wasn't a pretty corpse, not at all. First off, I drove up to the ranch house. Elaine wasn't there, so I went down to the bunkhouse and used the phone in Paco's room. I didn't bother with the niceties—I called the operator and told her to get the cops, and the cops got there fast, considering the distances. The highway patrol arrived in forty-five minutes and the sheriff not long after that.

"Where'd it happen?" asked the highway patrol officer from behind his man-with-no-eyes sunglasses. I told him.

"Do you want me to show you?" I asked.

"Later," he said, taking notes.

Then Elaine drove up in her car, followed by Paco's San Antonio buddy, the guy with the crewcut and the beige black-walled Ford.

Elaine lifted the sunglasses off her face. Maybe her eyes looked a little puffy, or maybe the puff was in my imagination. She came on cool, calm, and dry—Ms. Deodorant Cold—she might be gorgeous but she had slimy entrails for a heart. She barely glanced at Paco's wasted body.

My stomach hurt and my eyes were puffy. I felt like kicked dog shit. "You know something, Elaine," I said to her, "you really are one cold bitch." She acted as if she hadn't heard me.

About two minutes later the sheriff's deputy told me I was under arrest. Shocked silly. I couldn't even speak.

"What the fuck for, man?" I finally managed to croak.

"Sus-spi-shun of murder," the deputy said quietly.

"Huh? You're kidding," I said. I looked at the deputy and decided he wasn't. There were three cops around me. "Okay, guys, you better get out the cuffs," I said, raising my fists, " 'cause when I shake out of this trance, I'm gonna want to slam someone's ugly face."

They put the cuffs on me.

I saw Elaine talking to her crewcut friend and another guy that looked like some kind of plainclothes cop. Were they arresting me because I'd told the rich bitch she was a mobile pile of heartless crap? Goddamn—what kind of laws do they have in this country?

I slid into the patrol car and kicked the metal cage that divided the front and rear seats. "Put this thing in gear and git," I told the cop.

"Where to, mister?" he replied with a smirk.

The highway patrolman with the hyper-reflective sunglasses got in beside me. "Your jail better be air-conditioned," I told him. "I got a bad case of anger."

He just grinned. "You do look a little hot around the ears," he remarked.

"That's 'cause I'm mad, asshole." I replied.

"Aw shit," the officer said to the cop in the front seat, "he's already settin' up an insanity defense." The other cop laughed.

So I sulked for three days and ate beans sopped by day-old corn muffins, munched on browning lettuce salads, and chewed on the worst grade of horseburgers you can feed to human beings, only I wasn't supposed to be quite human, was I, me being a jailed criminal and all?

Then Thursday morning rolled around, and after the deputy on duty—his name was Ike—finished watching Phil Donahue, he put a fresh stick of Juicy Fruit in his mouth, moseyed down the short hall from his office, and opened my cell.

"Wail, Billy," he smiled, "seems you're out." He walked back down the hall in time to catch an ABC News Update. One of those beauty queens and blond-type journalists was talking about Qadaffi and Libya.

"Thanks for sounding so thrilled," I said. I didn't have anything against Ike or any of the cops for that matter. Ike made good instant coffee and he passed it around.

We were standing in the front office. The blonde blinked her blue eyes and talked about unemployment.

"You gotta sign a receipt sayin' you didn't get brutalized or hit with a wet rope," Ike said. His long bony hand pointed toward a blue form near the typewriter. His eyes stayed on the tube.

"Fuck no, I won't sign it, not until I talk to a lawyer."

Deputy Ike looked away from the TV set. The blonde had disappeared, replaced by an ad for freeze-dried potatoes. "Where do you think you're gonna get a lawyer?"

I shrugged. "Houston, San Antonio. I'll find me some ACLU radical."

The deputy guffawed and rocked back in his metal chair. "Shit. Those silly bastards only defend Mexicans who've shot Anglos. You're in the wrong skin, mister. 'Sides, you've been cleared."

"I figured that out. But that's the whole goddamn point. You accuse me of shooting my best friend, then you keep me incommunicado—that means, not talking to anyone in case you're as dumbshit as you seem—for three fuckin' days, three long fuckin' days. Then you let me go, just like that. It's some sorry bullshit, man—don't you know we got a Constitution?"

"Hey. Weren't you treated nice?" Ike grinned. I couldn't help liking the guy's go-along, get-along sense of the preposterous. He took my wallet out of a drawer, along with a baggy that held my buck knife and some change.

"Who decided to arrest me?" I asked, trying to sound half cool.

The deputy shrugged. "Who knows? We had a murderee, so we had to find us a murderer. You were pretty handy."

"Okay, wiseass. Why'd you let me out?"

Deputy Ike picked up a three-hole notebook and flipped a page. "Just got this about twenty minutes ago. FBI ballistics report. Your carbine hadn't been shot in several months."

"You don't need a lab to tell you that," I said.

The deputy flipped to another page. "Your carbine's a 30-caliber M-1. The bullet—which was recovered through the efforts of highly skilled crime fighters, meaning me— was a thirty-thirty round, most likely fired from a lever- action saddle gun with octagonal barrel. The bullet was a dum-dum, but you might've guessed that, given the size of the exit wound." He shut the notebook. "The sheriff told me to free yah after the report came in."

"When'd he tell you that?"

Deputy Ike grinned. "Well, that's classified information, but it does seem like—to the trained observer—like some- one wanted you to cool out a couple of days, and seein' as we didn't have any visitors, I guess they decided we were a pretty cheap hotel."

Yeah. I smelled Elaine Masterson and a case of the rich man's law. Well, goddamn.

I sat down on a stool by the water fountain and went through my wallet. Everything was there. Okay, what's the use in screaming at the cop? Elaine and I needed to talk—one former employee to one former employer.

"By the way, Buchanan, 'fore I forget. You're supposed to pick up an envelope next door in the clerk's annex. Just next door. Out the front and take a right."

"Thanks for the coffee," I said as I opened the front door and didn't wait for a reply.

The dumpy clerk with the dyed-blond beehive hairdo gave me a friendly smile, then asked me if I was growing a beard for Western Round-up Days. I said no ma'am, they didn't let me use a shaver in jail 'cause I might commit genocide or slash up the deputies' porno magazines.

"Then you must be Mr. Buchanan," she replied, un- fazed. "I think I have something in the safe for you. Please wait." She left the counter and went into a back room. A sixtyish gray-haired woman stepped out of the back, looked at me with a pair of limp blue eyes, then sighed. She returned to the back room. I checked out the calendar supplied by the local farm implements company—Bison Brothers, their logo a double-headed buffalo—then looked for my reflection in the hard-waxed white linoleum floor. The beehive reappeared. "Here you go Mr. Buchanan," she said, starting to hand me a legal-size manila envelope. "No—please let me see some identification first." I sniggered and fished my Michigan driver's license out of my wallet. She glanced at the license, then gave me the envelope. "Good-bye," she said breezily as I walked out the door.

"Bye, ma'am," I said, turning to tip my black cowboy hat.

Once out on the sidewalk, I opened the envelope. It held six hundred bucks in crisp one-hundred-dollar bills and a note typed on a piece of R. P. Masterson Enterprises stationery.

"Bill B.—Thanks for your assistance. Your services are no longer required.—E. M."

Six hundred tax-free bucks for two weeks' work. Like hell. She should have been paying me for my stint in jail, the bitch. And the note. I'd planned on quitting, not getting fired. My thoughts short-circuited. I looked across the courthouse square and slapped the envelope against my palm, just as a steel blue XKE rolled to a stop in front of me.

"Need a ride, cowboy?"

It was Anne Davis, alone, with a fetching smile and no Turk.

My thoughts short-circuited one more time.

"What're you doing here?"

She gunned the Jag's engine, then let it idle. "Oh, I don't know ... I think I've been waiting for you to get out of jail."

I leaned against the car door and brought my face near Anne's. "Where are you planning on going?" I asked.

"Hong Kong. Tokyo. Anyplace that accepts American Express."

She reached across the car and unlocked the other door. I went around and got in. My Resistol wouldn't fit, so I set it behind the top of the bucket seat.

Anne turned on the car's air conditioner. I was glad she did.

And I didn't ask her any probing sociological questions or any egghead existential questions or any silent psycho-analytic questions, and I didn't ask her anything else fancy and multisyllabic since those phrases constitute my entire vocabulary of college horseshit.

And I'll never bad-mouth a Holiday Inn again, not ever. She already had the keys and a couple of buckets of ice and a bottle each of bourbon, scotch, gin, and tonic water. Right on. Even the bed sheets were turned down. What a hustler.

Her athletic body fought the pleasant fight of touch, re-sistance, moving its own motion, then driving with me to a long supple climax.

She kissed me on my cheek, tickling her lips on my scraggy beard. "Want to watch television?" she asked.

"No," I said, half-exhausted, my face in the pillow.

"Then you better get some more energy, kid." She kissed me on the neck, on my side, then on my thigh. Ten minutes later we made love again.

"Hey, I got to know something," I said, maybe a half hour after our third go-round.

She was out of the bed, looking at her body in the dresser mirror. "Do you think my breasts are too small?" she asked, cupping her breasts in her hands and examin-ing them, then looking once more in the mirror.

"I don't rate stuff like that," I said.

"Oh?" She sat down on the chair beside the bed and

poured herself another belt of bourbon and ice. "Jarret always said my breasts were too small. You don't like big breasts?"

"I didn't say that. I'm into rating breasts on a different scale, that's all."

She looked at me carefully. "What scale's that?"

"Kissability. In that field you're on the top of the stack."

She laughed and leaned back in the chair, sipping her drink. "I knew you were sexist scum," she said with a giggle. She let her head rest on the top of the chair.

I looked at her. She wore a faraway face, a face with a superficial smile, a lurking vanity, eyes that saw the ceiling as a fog. "Hey," I said, "I gotta know something."

She snapped back from her thoughts. "What's that?"

"How come you were waiting for me?"

She took a small sip of bourbon, a drop of the liquor clinging to her upper lip. "Don't ask."

"Got to ask," I said.

"How come?"

I rubbed my beard with my palm, then winked. "Why, otherwise I might think you're some sort of creep."

She didn't know whether I meant it as a joke. Suddenly I didn't know what I'd meant either. She put her glass down.

There was a pause in both of us.

"I don't know," she said. "You were so nice last Sunday. I heard you were in jail, and I decided yesterday I'd drive down here and see you. I called the sheriff's office to find out if there were any visiting hours, and they told me you'd be getting out this morning."

"They told you that yesterday?"

"Yes."

"When for chrissakes?"

She shrugged. "About noon maybe, a little before. They didn't tell you?"

I shook my head slowly and saw my dumbfounded face

reflected in the dresser mirror, a portrait of redneck confusion. "Can't figure out why they didn't either."

"Going to raise a stink?"

"I don't know." I reached over the side of the bed and picked up my gin and tonic. "So that's it then. You thought I was nice."

"Nice is enough. Most men I know are selfish assholes."

"Yeah, men tend to be like women, don't they?"

She winced. "And you've got a nice body," she said.

"Yeah, that's what they tell me."

"Who tells you that?" she asked sarcastically.

"The women," I said.

"The women who are assholes?"

"Now hold on lady. I didn't say that."

"No," she replied, taking another sip of whiskey, "but I did."

We didn't have a whole hell of a lot left to say. No, I wasn't a dream cowboy—but I wasn't a complete mistake either.

I talked her into driving me back to Chorillo, which took some effort because it was the wrong direction, seeing that she wanted to drive back to Corpus Christi. Anne said she had a huge villa right there on the bay, over the blue green bay, as she put it, and I should stop by, come see her sometime, sometime real soon, after I cleared up whatever it was I'd been doing at the Masterson place. "You'll like the waves," she said, "all that water and the sun."

On the trip to Chorillo I tried to pump her for info about Elaine. Yes, she'd known Elaine Masterson a long time. They'd gone to high school together, in Houston. Elaine was a couple of years older. The Mastersons were old money—cattle money that turned into oil. Seems Elaine's grandfather once had a share of a West Texas ranch that sat on a small Saudi Arabia. Out in the Permian Basin somewhere. But the Mastersons weren't as wealthy as they used to be—bad management, something about foreign investments, Anne didn't know for sure. Why was I interested? Had I been in bed with Elaine? Shit, I told her, conversations just leap from money to sex. And back, Anne said. Then I asked about the Turk, and she said he'd been recommended as a bodyguard by a friend in Houston, an independent oilman with operations in Indonesia and the Middle East. She'd rented him just to scare Jarret.

"Didn't work too well, did it?" she mused.

"If he'd been sober, Jarret would have seen him and probably have split."

"Yeah, Jarret's chicken like that."

"Did you know your bodyguard had been a cop?" I asked Anne, taking a chance.

She looked at me with surprise. "He told me he once worked for Interpol but he didn't want me to tell anybody."

"How come?"

"Uh ... he said he'd made a lot of long-distance enemies."

"What kind of cop was he?"

"What do you mean?"

"Like, did he bust people for drugs."

"That I do not know," she said. "Where'd you hear he was a cop?"

"From Paco."

"Who?"

"Paco Ramirez—my boss. The guy I was supposed to have shot."

"Why would he know Rudi?"

"Seems he knew a lot of people," I said, thinking it was a dumb thing to say but still wanting to say it. We were almost to Chorillo. "Hey, you sure you can't take me out to the ranch?"

"Thought we had an agreement. That'd take another

half hour out and another half hour back. I really *do* have to be back in Corpus." She was adamant.

"Okay. I'll work out something."

I gave her a kiss as I got out of the car, and she frenched me, right in front of the Source Oil Company gas station.

Kirt the mechanic saw us, and the kid blushed from beneath his grease stains, then turned and went back into the automotive bay.

"Watch yourself," Anne said, touching my cheek. Maybe we did have some more to say. She drove out of the station and headed back up the highway.

"Hey, Kirt." The boy had watched the short good-bye from inside the station office. I walked toward the door.

"Hi, mister. I'm sorry, uh," he stammered, "I thought you all might want some gas." He looked at me for a moment. "Say, you *are* Mr. Buchanan. I heard you were arrested."

I nodded. "Yeah, but it didn't stick. How's the gas business?"

"Slow. Always slow in this town." Kirt picked up a can of Gojo and started rubbing the grease cleaner from his hands. "Real sorry about Paco, just real sorry."

"I am too. Great guy."

"You all seemed to get along sort of fast," Kirt said hesitantly.

"Yeah," I agreed. "We were in the same unit in Nam. Guess it meant something to both of us. He gave me a job."

"Oh, was *that* it?" Kirt tilted his head in a curious way, like a final answer had just slid into a slot.

The kid's response puzzled me. "Why do you sound so surprised?"

Kirt gave a loose shrug. "I dunno . . . ole Blaine, I guess."

"Blaine?"

"Yeah. He kept sayin' you were another one of Paco's sneakin' big city buddies. You were friends in Vietnam?"

"Didn't know him there. The Eleventh Cav's a big regiment and half the time it was spread all over hell. Almost literally."

"And you two just bumped into one another."

"I run into guys that were in the Cav all the time. It's happened before and it'll happen again. We were in the same shitpile for a while and it marked us."

"Sort of like bein' on the same team, huh?"

"Yeah, I guess. Now what's the deal with Blaine?"

Kirt shook his head and turned around, looking for a dry rag to wipe his hands on. He found one. "I dunno. Mr. Rawlins is a strange sort of man, I think," Kirt said, raising an eyebrow. "He's got a streak of mean in him wide enough to drive on." Kirt tossed the rag in a trash can. "You wan'a soda, mister?"

I said yeah and gave Kirt the money for both of us. He thanked me and got himself a Dr Pepper. I ordered a Seven-up. "Blaine work on the Dickson place a long time?" I asked.

"Not down here," Kirt said, shaking his head. "Oh, I hear he's worked for ole Dickson a good while, up near Corsicana or somewhere in East Texas, but he just come down here a year ago."

"What about Bennet?"

"Now there's a critter. Used to be a real nice kind of man, but got to drinkin' real bad."

"How long ago?"

"Oh, long 'fore Blaine showed up. Man, Bennet didn't have a dime, ever. Wife divorced him about five years ago 'cause he was a drunk. He didn't have nothin' for child support. Always used to complain to me about child support, how bad it was. And me being barely eleven." Kirt grinned. "Bennet would be so drunk he wouldn't know whose side I was on."

"How old are you now, Kirt?"

"Nearly fifteen."

"Well, almost grown," I said. "Okay, Bennet's a drunk."

Kirt sat down on a metal folding chair beside the cash register. "Long comes Blaine to run the ranch and Bennet's got a new Buick and fancy western clothes from Cutter Bill's." Kirt took another swig of soda and looked at me. I just nodded. Kirt smiled. "These men around here think I'm sort of slow," he said, touching his temple with his finger. "Everybody 'cept Archibald. He knows better."

I cleared my throat. "So Bennet comes into some money?" Kirt nodded. "About the time Blaine comes down from another Dickson ranch?" Kirt nodded again. "Okay, boy—and what else is bothering you?"

Kirt scratched his head. "Six months later Paco shows up."

"Hey, I thought Paco was from around here."

"Oh he is—or was. He was gone for a long time. But it's not just him that shows up. All these other smart guys from San Antonio, and that good-looking Masterson woman, they all show up, like there's a gold rush or something." Kirt raised both of his eyebrows.

"And?" I asked.

Kirt shook his head. "It all adds up to me, and then it don't add up to me." He finished off the soft drink. "You believe in UFOs, Mr. Buchanan?"

"No."

"Neither do I. But I tell you what, there's a lot of funny flying shit that comes up from Mexico." He didn't say anything else.

I didn't like the silence. "What do you mean?"

Kirt stood up and walked over to the door, looking at the highway. "I just got me a picture, Mr. Buchanan, in my head. Bennet still gets crocked and he comes around here and talks about re-tiring and moving to Marble Falls. He talks about joining a country club and playing golf, and he's never played golf in his life. Now where you gonna get money for that, I ask him, for retiring. And he just snorts like he snorts, and so I ask again where's he gonna get the money, and he says, why, from the sky son, from the sky, then he giggles like the drunk he is. At least he don't get mean when he's drunk like Blaine does." Kirt spit out the front door, then looked at me. "What do you make of it, mister?"

I thought a moment. "Nothin'."

"You mean you don't give a shit."

"I didn't say that. So what happened after Paco showed up?"

"You know, I really shouldn't complain about this so much. Ever since Blaine and Paco have been here, we do get a better grade of people for customers. Why, Lieutenant Colonel Stewart L. Harrison shows up now and then."

"Who's that?"

"The deputy commander of the Texas Department of Public Safety."

"The state cops?"

"Yeah."

"What's he doing here?"

"I don't know, but he doesn't come around in a police car," Kirt winked. "He drives through here in his own car, or somebody's private car. It's a brand-new Lincoln Mark VI."

"How do you know he's a big state cop?"

Kirt gave a sly grin. "He buys gas on a state credit card with his name on it."

I let out a little whistle. "You're a dangerous young man, Kirt." I thought for a moment. "What's Harrison look like? Mid-thirties with a crewcut?" I had a bead on Paco's friend in the beige Ford.

"No. Old feller, long gray hair, longer than any state cops I've ever seen 'ceptin him."

"Who do you think he's going to see?"

Kirt shook his head from side to side. "I don't know. I don't ask questions Mr. Buchanan, I just look and listen."

"Then why are you talking to me?"

The kid smiled. "Aw c'mon. Ain't you really a government agent or something?"

"Me?"

"Don't deny it."

"Hey kid, I do deny it. Where'd you get a screwy idea like that?"

Kirt looked at me, scrutinizing every twitch. One had to be careful with this young man 'cause he knew more than just which wrenches went where. "You really aren't a cop?"

"Nope."

"But you'd lie to me if you were a cop."

"I'm not lying. Have I done anything cop-like? I got fuckin' arrested."

Kirt looked at me intently. "Blaine come by here this morning and asked me if I'd seen you."

"So?"

"I told him you'd been arrested."

I shrugged my shoulders. "Yeah?"

"He said that's one cop's way of getting out another."

"What?"

Kirt went back to his metal chair, thought about sitting down, then just put his hands in his pockets. "Don't ask me to explain what Blaine said."

"I don't think you have to. Did Blaine say anything about Paco?"

Kirt nodded. "Said that was another dead spic cop, as far as he was concerned."

"And what'd Blaine say he'd been doing?" I did some fast calculations on my own.

"Blaine said he'd been away all weekend, down somewheres in the valley, 'round Harlingen. And he just told me that outright, funny like, like he'd memorized it or something." Kirt grinned again. "You following me?"

I raised my own eyebrows. "Yup."

Kirt took a deep breath. "Yeah, Blaine's got a streak of mean." I asked the boy to get us both another soda. "Okay, but I buy this time," he said firmly.

"Tell me one more thing, will you, Kirt?"

"Sure."

"About Elaine Masterson."

"What about her?"

"Anything. Just tell me anything you know."

"Well, she moved here six months ago ... and she's a nasty woman."

"She moved here?"

"Just before Paco came back."

"And that's another one of those coincidences that get in your head?"

"Yeah. Nothin' much ever happens around here. May as well pay close attention to what does."

"Did she just buy the ranch?"

"Don't know. Far's I know her family already owned it. I hear she's rich folks though, from Dallas."

"I heard she was from Houston."

"Dallas, Houston, Chicago. They're all big cities. And I ain't been to any of 'em."

"Do you want to?"

Kirt lowered his head and seemed to look at his feet. "I'd like to see something else sometime. After high school maybe. I don't know."

I gave the kid a pat on the back. "You're bright. Which means you better keep your mouth shut for a while. You want a barbecue sandwich?"

"Where from. Archie's?"

"Yeah."

"Can't get one there. He's gone for a couple of weeks.

Miz Archibald hauled him off to Kerrville. She keeps tal-
kin' retirement, and she's finally got him by the ear. I'm
not too hungry anyway."

I looked across the highway at Millie's store and decided that I wasn't all that hungry either. "I'll be back in
about five minutes, Kirt. You want a fried pie?"

"A cold one from Millie's or a hot one from La Fiesta?"

"I was going to get a cold one."

"That'd be nice," he said.

"Say, uh, do you think you can drive me out to the
Masterson Ranch?"

The kid said no. "I can't leave, not 'til eight. 'Sides, I
don't have a car and I don't have a driver's license." He
gave another one of his sly smiles. "But I don't let the license business stop me when I've got wheels."

I told him that I didn't think he was the kind of kid that
would.

Millie was jawing on the phone with some friend in San
Diego, at least that was the way it sounded. She hung up
when I came to the counter, and told me that she'd just got
all the gossip from "up county." Seems I got picked up at
the jail by a woman in a fancy car. That true? I said yes.
"Thought it'd be," she said, "Lou Ann's gossip's usually
accurate. So what do you need?"

I found a fried pie and put it on the counter. "You got a
canteen for sale?" I asked.

"What kind? Army or one with a shoulder strap?"

"Does the army kind have a pistol belt?" She said yes,
she could sell me a pistol belt. "Then I'll take a service
canteen," I replied. "Say, do you have a sheath for a buck
knife like this one?" I showed her my blade.

She told me to hold on, then she went and got a card-
board box and started rummaging through the carton.
"How's this one?" she asked, producing a used black
leather sheath. "You'll have to carry the knife folded, but
that's the way you're supposed to, isn't it?"

I unhitched my trousers and slid the sheath around to my right side. The buck fit the sheath to a T. Attaching the canteen cover to the pistol belt, I adjusted the belt, fitting it high on my waist so the knife wasn't trapped between the belt and my side. I didn't want to deal with any blisters.

"You taking a hike?" Mildred asked.

"Yeah."

"You gonna be stayin' at the Masterson place?"

Hmmm. She had a set of questions and she seemed to be the local gossip columnist. "No. I'm gonna be leaving."

"How soon?"

"Tomorrow. Then that's it."

"And where are you going from here?"

"I don't know. New Mexico, maybe L.A. But I'm gonna leave this town to the natives. By the way, do you have any large manila envelopes?"

"How many do you need?"

"Uh, three. I need some writing paper, too. And you got any stamps?"

Mildred nodded. "Yup. Post office moves over here when the Archibalds is gone."

"Gimme a dozen for domestic postage." She complied.

I went back across the highway to the gas station. Kirt was in the back of the mechanics bay sitting by a creaking fan. "Here's your pie, son," I said. He muttered a thanks. "Hey, what's the matter, Kirt?"

Kirt looked at his shoes, then he looked at the fan. "I ain't told all that stuff to no one before."

"So?"

"Well . . . so. So what if . . . what if I'm just foolin' myself into thinking that something real is happening? What if . . . what if I come up with a story?" He looked at me sort of sorrowful-like. "Let's say I come up with a story 'cause . . . 'cause I sit in a dirty little place every day 'cept when I have to ride a school bus up to Freer?"

I told him I didn't understand.

He just looked at me. "I guess you don't, do you?"

"Kirt. Don't start getting mopey. You've got nothing to worry about. Not at all."

"I don't get mopey, 'cept when my mom's coughing up her lungs." He leaned back in the chair he sat in, and put his hands behind his head. The fan beat circles of wind in the air. "So, Mr. Buchanan, you think I've really seen something."

"I think you've really hit on something that's still happening, Kirt. And I'm going to find out if you're right—and if the whole thing fits."

He looked half-startled, then he cracked his knuckles. "I figured you might." The boy hunched forward in the chair. "I figured lots of times I'd go do something, too."

"Naw," I said, pointing a finger at him, "you stay put. It's better that way, believe me. Hey, you got a pencil?" He pulled one out of his front pocket, and I jotted down a note to Cousin Pete and one to Aunt Doe, then addressed the envelopes. "Say, where's the john around here?" I asked.

" 'Round back." He gave a motion with his hand.

"I'll be right back," I said.

I went around to the rear of the gas station and went in the rest room. I slipped three one-hundred-dollar bills in Doe's letter, three in Pete's, and then I added a PS to Pete's note, asking him to use the money for helping out Aunt Doe, if he didn't hear from me in, say, a month? I sealed the envelopes, put stamps on them, took a piss, then came back to the bay.

"Kirt, I want you to do something for me. See these envelopes? I want you to mail them—put them on the mail truck yourself. Got any problems with that?" He shook his head no. "And here's twenty bucks for you." I pulled out my wallet and gave the kid two tens, leaving me three ones in cash reserve.

"Why are you giving me twenty bucks? I'd do it for nothing."

I winked. "You just mail the letters." I gave the two addressed envelopes to him. "And don't say anything about them, okay?"

"Okay."

I held up the third envelope. "Now listen to me. You know the Masterson place at all?"

"Not a'tall."

"Well, about a quarter mile past the main house there's a bunkhouse and a barn. Behind the bunkhouse and next to the barn is a woodpile. If you don't hear from me in a week, you get out to that woodpile. There'll be a pack in it near the top, left-hand side, and this envelope will be in it and have your name written right here on the back."

Kirt's eyes were as big as hazel green bumblebees. "Gosh," he said, the gosh that a fifteen-year-old is still capable of saying when he still means gosh and not goddamn. "What am I supposed to do . . . after that?"

"Keep your mouth shut and keep what you find. Including the pack." I smiled at the kid.

He didn't smile back. He didn't know what the whole story was. "Why . . . why're you doing this?"

"Doing what ?"

"What you're doing?"

I laughed. I laughed at myself. "Blaine's got a streak of mean in him."

Then the kid took me by surprise. He shook his head, looked at me incredulously, then looked at the slow revolving fan. "I guess he ain't the only one that's got one, is he, Mr. Buchanan?"

I laughed again. This time at the boy. And I made the laughter stick. "Ever pull a piece of meat out of the goo that used to be your friend's back, huh, Sherlock?"

The boy told me he only sort of understood.

I told him he was lucky.

We shook hands when I left. It took me three hours and half a canteen to jog and strut the thirteen miles from Chorillo to the Masterson Ranch. I paused only once, at the bridge over Quivara Creek, and there I took a leak into the dry sand, from the wooden bridge into the soaking dust. Must have looked ridiculous. Thirteen miles in three hours. I set a good clip, given the heat and all, and stayed at it, glad I had my cowboy hat but sorry that the thing was wicked black. Boy, can that un-color absorb heat and then put it to your head.

But I felt good, glad to be out of the cell. Ace had so much energy he broad-jumped one of the cattle guards. The second time I tried it I slipped when I landed and I bumped hell out of my leg. Well, no more tricks.

Every so often I'd wash the coat of dust off my lips and tongue, but the walk wasn't all that bad, not at all that bad. The yucca and prickly pear filled the landscape, between the mesquite and the sparse oak and, yes, the insistent stretch of dust and fist-size stone.

I didn't see a car parked in front of the ranch house, but I went to the backdoor anyway and checked inside. Nothing. Nobody home. Paco's pickup was parked behind the bunkhouse. I went and looked inside the cab. Keys in the ignition. I popped open the glove compartment. Hotdog—expert criminologists? What kind of cops were on this case? The .357 Magnum lay on top of a stack of roadmaps and paper crap, the flashlight in back of it. Thorough investigations? Double horseshit.

The keys to the bunkhouse were beneath the potted cactus. I went in and lay the pistol on the counter, then washed my face. Christ, let's get some air conditioner in here. I flicked on the switch, but the damn thing failed to start. And the lights didn't kick on either. I didn't bother checking the fuse box, I went straight to the meter. Yeah, shut off. So be it.

By my watch it was five to five, so I still had sunlight and the extra flashlight in the utility closet, if it was still there. It was. In my room I found a change of clothes lying jumbled on the bed. I always fold everything. So I did a fast inventory. Somebody'd gone through my things that was obvious, but nothing seemed to be missing. My five hundred extra bucks was still hidden behind the box of Arm and Hammer baking soda below the kitchen sink.

Well, I thought, last things first. I put the money in the manila envelope and wrote: "To Kirt c/o Source Oil Chorillo." I didn't know the kid's last name, did I? Big deal. I took an extra pair of shorts and a change of socks out of my rucksack and stuffed everything in it, except toothbrush and toothpaste, then took the sack and envelope out to the woodpile. Tucking the envelope into the waterproof fly of the sack's flap, I tied all the ties and buttoned all the buttons. I removed about a half-dozen logs, stuck the pack in the crevice, then replaced the wood. Even the rats wouldn't suspect anything about this woodpile.

I looked toward the ranch house, half-expecting to see a human-size rodent, female version.

I found a bottle of tequila in Paco's closet. His room had been picked through pretty well. A couple of books lay on the floor—mysteries, something on sociology—and an odd assortment of magazines. *Business Week, Better Homes and Gardens?* I wanted to find his new shotgun, with some 12-gauge deer shot, but when you really need it, you can't even buy that kind of luck.

Lying flat on the floor beneath Paco's bed was a brass picture frame holding a photo of Madre—black Indian eyes and turquoise necklace. I took the picture into the living room and opened the window shade. What a hard-soft woman she seemed to be, the black and the gray in her hair. Sunset was still a good two hours away. I watched the sky redden a moment, then placed the frame upright beneath the table lamp.

The Dos Equis in the frige still felt cool to the touch, but whoever had shut off the electricity had forgotten that ice melts and lettuce goes rotten. I tossed the vegetables out, mopped up some of the water, then tried to find a church key. Can't ever find an opener when you need one, I said, but then, most American brews have gone to twist-offs. I rummaged through the drawers and looked on top of the refrigerator, moving an empty fruit bowl and a can of green peas.

It wasn't a bottle opener I found—it was an eye opener, a big photograph, or four pieces of a big photograph, black-and-white aerial, high resolution. And I recognized the target area—the Dickson Ranch, the one next door.

So I used my knife to pry off the bottle cap, then moved into the living room with beer and photo, sinking into a rocking chair. I put the picture into one ragged piece. There was the main ranch house and a long covered walkway leading to what, the maid's quarters? Out front was a road with a couple of cars and trucks parked at odd angles. Behind the ranch house and a thick grove of trees were several barns, or long stables, and most of all, the first of all, was a big circle made with an orange grease pencil and the word "Hah!" written above the upper curve of the circle. In the upper right-hand corner of the photo was a big orange "S" and a tiny arrow pointing up. So south was toward the roof—well, I was oriented.

Inside the orange circle was what appeared to be rocks and trees and shadows of other trees and rocks, not too many but enough large ones so that the only kind of plane that could land in the field would be a kamikaze. Which was a puzzling thought, using that large field as a runway, because topographically there wasn't anyplace else a sane pilot could have landed the high-winged single-engine aircraft parked between two of the rear barns. Curiouser and curiouser, I thought. A plane that size, maybe a Piper Cub, might be able to take off from the narrow strip of land edging the main road for fifteen hundred feet or so, just maybe. But near those barns was a strange place to park a plane if your airfield was five hundred feet away and on the other side of a fence line. "Hah!" is right. I folded the photo pieces, put them in my pocket, and looked at the picture of Madre.

I fell asleep, maybe from the sunburn I got in the afternoon, though it wasn't too bad a burn, seeing that I had a pretty deep tan to me.

I woke up in darkness, stretched, then went out on the porch. A fresh breeze from the east moved the half-moon's light through the trees. It was past midnight. I had really conked out and without one drop of tequila. Well, I hadn't planned on moving out tonight anyway. Weren't there still some things to check out?

But why move until I had talked to Elaine Masterson? I might be an ungreased cog in a well-oiled machine if— and a big if as far as I was emotionally concerned—she had something to do with all of this.

No, maybe it wasn't such a goddamn big if.

When I looked at the stars, they held their hard light for a half twinkle, then, with the breeze, they too shook like an uncertainty.

The distant bark of a lone night dog rasped across the open land, cutting through the scrub with a certain driven, yet ragged edge. Kie-yote, I muttered. Getting by on the rim, with the dumps and trash bags and the hounds and the moon. The moon. Oh shit, I said.

The coyote's second howl, as if nearer, began like a moan, deep moan, then turned upon itself—a rise in pitch toward a dark, sudden laugh.

And I'll to bed on that, I said to myself.

# 9

EARLY IN THE MORNING, sevenish, I discovered the phone still worked. The dial tone sounded lonely. I buzzed Anne Davis's number in Corpus. No answer. The ring sounded lonelier. But why expect something different? Maybe she'd found herself a new candidate for dream cowboy, or a ragtime musician, y'know, piano man and say hey, Mr Bones, with a huffy American voice? I took another sip of coffee. Now why would I think she'd go after a musician? Hmmm. She'd tasted like a woman in search of rhythm, and I don't mean just backbone motion or deep vibration in the hips. I couldn't fix the thought for sure, but there'd been something in the way she'd made love, something necessary, something jagged, like a broken song that even a morning later tore through the brain orbits.

I shut down the propane stove. There was enough gas in the tank outside to last another six months. Who'd be around to burn it? Paco wouldn't. Me neither.

I stepped out on the porch and yawned. A pair of needle-nosed pliers were sitting on one of the window sills. Hadn't noticed them before. Well, probably Paco's, a leftover from a B.S. in E.E. I picked up the pliers and opened and closed them like they were a toothless pair of calipered jaws. Click—a clean bite of air, a hold on nothing. Yes. Click. Something else was buzzing around my brain, something very different from Anne Davis, a buzz that gave no satisfaction, loose ideas that circled bird-like, buzzard-like—that's it, I thought as I drove the truck out toward the ridge, thoughts moving buzzard-like, as if one of those ugly birds cutting figure eights in the air had started to patrol my brain case.

I reached the ridge, got out, and wandered up the fence line, through the mesquite and along the path I'd scrambled four days earlier. The murder scene had been pretty well picked through, beaten down by cop boots and the like. I followed the path of several pairs onto Dickson land, feeling a little naked, half-watched as I walked across the broken dirt, paused, and walked on until I reached the tree line. No doubt about it. A rifle, with or without a scope, could pick off anything along the ridge, and if the murderer moved a little ways up the knoll, he'd be able to shoot clear to where the truck was parked.

Okay, so what. The tree line had already been good and stomped through, everyone else had checked this angle, everyone and everything. A buzzard, making its looping arcs and eights in the sky, took a glide path down, landing on a dead oak. It sat there, fat, ragged, gray, and ugly, swinging its hangdog head. I put my Magnum's sights on the bird, then decided not to shoot—I wasn't after a bag of feathers, I knew that, and I wasn't about to raise Cain on the Dickson by opening fire too soon. I wished to God I had that carbine. In all likelihood the ballistics lab still had it tucked away.

Back at the truck I found a matchbook on the ground. "Bexar County Sheriff's Posse." Somebody'd been down from San Antone. I'd been around long enough to know that Bexar was pronounced like bear, and for some reason I liked the word because it was a surprise. I struck one of the matches and it lit. So dry—four days on the ground and not even a touch of dew. Too dry.

Naw, I said out loud, time for me to bag it, get to my own kind of zone. Fernando, Joe? Where the hell had they gone to? I slipped the matchbook in my pocket. Who the hell were they anyway? And Elaine Masterson. If she'd been a man, I'd have punched her out by now, just for being a snob. But she wasn't a man, and that, to me, to my mind, to my body, was an inescapable fact. I saw her face again. Gosh—my own private kind of gosh. I'd better admit it to myself and get it out of the system 'cause not admitting it could be poison. Yeah. In my back brain I still wanted her, if only for one night. Maybe that was why Ace was hanging around, waiting for a slim thread I might follow into the sack. But cul-de-sac's more like it. She was impossible. Dead end, box canyon, Paco shot through the chest and I still got a woman on the mind. Did I care about a murdered friend or did I care about getting laid? I wasn't quite sure and I felt like a louse.

I knew I had to know why Paco'd died.

So no wonder I can't think my way out of this hole, I said to myself as I turned the truck and pointed it up the draw toward the twenty-square corral. Nothing had changed around there either. A piece of aluminum siding lay on the ground and brown grass, looking like some kind of space wreckage dropped to earth. I tossed the piece into the corral and kicked one of the posts. Sure was sturdy—well, I'd sunk them deep.

I drove off again, brain still buzzing, this time like the fly in the cab. I took a swipe at the black bit of noise and missed. The second shot mashed the insect to the windshield. One out of two—guess those old Snake pilot eyeballs were still semicalibrated, gunsight like, as in bang and zap him. Then I laughed at myself—shit, all I'd done was nail a fly when what I needed to nail was an idea, an idea that seemed to be beyond me. The truck drove on automatic pilot, my body going through all the motions and the eyes going through all the seeing, but the mental pattern not one of complete motor consciousness. Damn. I was heading toward the southwest corner and the small corral. Well, why not?

From the place I stopped, you could see the corral's back end, a corral next to the edge of nowhere, a corral barely big enough to stick two cows in side to side. What a useless waste of energy, I'd thought as I was putting it in, really a waste of assets, muscle, and time. But I'm not paid to think, right? That's how I had rationalized it.

Unusual? The gate, which faced the valley, was painted a camouflage spray of green and brown. Five feet from one of the corner posts I found the black power cable, then heard a click and a faint electric buzz.

Now don't ever stand in front of a buzzing gate—it's likely to be a radar, and if it is, you're sterilized.

Radar, angled slats, no tilt—an economy-size phased array? Why be that complex? I located a pair of lifters, set in those puzzling concrete holes. So the gate could rise, maybe six to eight inches, and turn on a ten-degree angle, just enough to get a good low-level read on the little valley, the one going north from Old Mexico.

This didn't take a calculating mind. I was looking at a radar trip wire for aircraft below Laredo's and San Antone's traffic control line of sight. Now I knew I was into someone's project—somebody's project, somebody so big it smelled like government, federal government.

Click and the buzz went off. I traced the black cable to a

relay pod and back into the brush to a transmitter. The buzz was a recharge noise, from a small, maybe four-kilo-watt generator, a quiet four kilowatts that looked micro-chip and megabucks. Someone sure wanted some fancy long-range security. Then I thought about other kinds of security, as in local, but I didn't find any trip wires or ground sensors that would pick up on my snooping around. This would have been a good place though for ground sensors, the Nam style that pick up VC tread and flash back to the world that Charlie's trying to sneak and peek—then bam, here comes the Cobra man.

Yeah, I had to respect the technology, though maybe the radar system seemed a little elaborate. Then I thought about the terrain. Maybe a tracker craft with look-down, see-down gear could cover that scoop, but that'd have been more expensive and stupider than this gate rig. Still, if you were trying to track a plane flying north, toward the Dicksons', let's say—I was at least trying to sound hypo-thetical—what would this give you, five or six minutes' notice? Maybe six, if you included the bank time and the touchdown, because the pilot highballing up this valley sure wasn't going to wait for a clear runway. But where would a plane the size of a B-25 land on the Dickson Ranch? Maybe the radar was just a big counting device, counting low-level penetrations, aircraft using this valley to get away from the border, then getting some altitude and heading for points north. Maybe, I said, but not damn likely. Five minutes was a lot of time if you were talking jet fighters, as in interception.

I was standing on a piece of green tarp when the back-ground buzz in my brain clicked off. Of course. So I drove back to the other corral, and in the brush, where Paco'd pointed, I found the stretch of tarp he'd pulled from the pickup the day he died. In a long metal tube, about half the diameter but twice as long as a scuba tank, I found a transmitter pod. Taped together, like a bunch of two-and-a-half-foot tent pegs, were three ground sensors. A little metal disposable ring ran around the bottom of the pod, its stenciling reading "DEA."

Drug Enforcement Administration? Death minus the TH. The three letters were an obvious kind of answer. Still I wanted to find a note, a personal explanation, but there was no script, just a label and the high-tech evidence.

Thinking about what I'd found—and about the hidden talents of Mr. Ramirez—I drove back to the ranch house. The Mercedes was now parked out in front. Elaine met me at the door.

"Thought you'd cleared out," she said from behind her sunglasses. She didn't sound sarcastic, just straightforward cool and matter-of-fact.

"Didn't know if you'd be needing me, Miz Masterson. For horse racing or fence mending."

"What do you mean. Didn't you get my note?"

"What note?" I lied.

"The one in the envelope with the six hundred dollars."

"I got the money, but I didn't see any note." Oh gee, I thought, why lie like this? Well, it was a chance to look at her up close, that was for sure.

"I wrote a note," she replied coldly, stepping back into the house. "We won't be requiring your assistance any longer."

"Shucks. Such a short job ... uh, how come?" I caught the screen door with my hand and stepped in after her. "Fernando and Joe coming back?"

She took off her sunglasses. We were in a cool hallway of dark red brick and Spanish tile, made darker by the move from sunlight to shade. "Yes ... that's it exactly. And when will you be leaving, now that you're no longer invited to stay?"

Christ—I was an inarticulate fool.

"Well, hell," I said, popping the screen door back open, "on the next bus out, lady."

She didn't give a damn about how angry I was. Her body wore the ice of perfect assurance.

"Good-bye," I said. I said it calmly.

"See you," she replied.

I stopped half way through the door. "Look, uh . . ."

"Yes?" And it was a yes from the dry Arctic of words.

Yes sir, she's out of my league. And I finally knew it. Then to hell with her—I had my game plan. "Look, it's almost midday. I won't be able to get a bus out 'til seven-thirty tomorrow morning. Can I spend the night in the bunkhouse? I'll clear out before, before dawn. Is one night's sleep such a pain?"

"Okay," she said, her lips somewhere between a thought and a smile, "but then you clear out. This isn't a charity organization I'm running." I agreed with that and said so. "Good, then I'm glad we're clear on something," she replied. "Is there anything else?"

I thought a second, sticking to the plan. "Yeah, uh, tomorrow morning, can I drive the pickup into Chorillo? I'll leave it with Kirt."

"Who?"

"The kid in the gas station."

"Fine," she shrugged. "Just don't steal it. If you do, you'll wish you hadn't."

"Theft's a crime in this county? Gee, I thought the only thing your pigs busted people for was smarting off to egotistical bitches."

I stepped out the door and slammed the screen.

She just laughed. "The threatened macho man. I knew I was going to have to get the bunkhouse fumigated."

"Fumigated? Who's that comment for, me or Paco? That trash line from your can of racist shit?"

"Racist shit?" Then she started a snicker that turned into a silence she couldn't fill. She looked at me. "Nope," she said, "not in the very least." Her last syllables disappeared in the slightest quiver of her jaw.

I felt stupid again and I wasn't sure why. And I wasn't angry. What could I say? "You know I didn't kill him," I said.

"I know," she nodded. "And neither did I."

I bit my lip. "Do you know who did?"

She stared at me for a moment. "Do you?" she asked, the cold edge back in her voice.

"No. Wish to God I did."

"If you find out, let me know." She opened the screen and offered me her hand. "Nice knowing you, Buchanan. Thanks for the fence work." I shook her hand and said it was all no bother. "By the way," she said, sounding almost friendly, "where'd you and Paco put the oxygen canisters?"

"The what?"

"You know, big bottles?" She described the tubes with her hands.

I knew she meant the transmitter pods. So she was in on the whole damn thing. "I don't follow you," I replied, sticking to my plan. "What're you talking about, stuff for an acetylene torch?"

"They might look like that. Yeah."

"Nope. Haven't seen a thing like'em, not on this ranch. What're you planning on using them for?"

"Gee," she smiled sweetly. "I don't know. I got a phone call from some supply house in San Antonio asking me when they'd be back." Her smile widened. God, she could lie real, *real* well.

So I'd stick to my plan, the loner's option, and let all the lying users play their own big-time game.

"Uh, I'll keep my eyes peeled ... for oxygen bottles."

She said good, then paused. "Say, what were you planning on doing with the rest of the afternoon?"

"Don't know. Nothin'. Sleeping maybe, getting ready to hit the road."

"Want to earn another day's pay?"

"For a half day's work?"

"For a couple of hours' work, at the most."

"You pay in advance?"

She smirked. "You take a check?"

"If they'll cash it in New Mexico."

"They'll cash my checks on the moon. Wait a second." She came back to the door and scribbled off a forty-dollar check drawn on the Bank of the Southwest in Houston. "What am I supposed to do for this?" I asked.

"Mow the lawn around the swimming pool. I'm going to have a party tomorrow night and it's looking weedy."

"That's it?"

"That's it." I said okay and took the check. "The mower's already out back," she added. "Gas can's in the garage." She went inside.

I drove down to the bunkhouse, parked the truck, and took off my shirt. In ten minutes I was spraying cut bermuda around the backyard and onto the pool, having a hell of a good time behind a mower that pounded like the son of a jackhammer. A half hour later the beige Ford with three men in it came off the rise and down the tree line. I lost sight of it, then saw it again as it made the last cattle guard and pulled in front of the house, disappearing once more.

When I finished the grass—maybe forty minutes later—I was sweating like the proverbial pig, just superhot and wet. So I took a short run, did a flop into the pool, and paddled around, relaxing.

I crawled out and walked to the front of the ranch house, shaking the water out of my hair. The beige Ford was gone and so was Elaine's Mercedes. Hey, I said to myself as I dumped my half-filled cowboy hat on my head, the water spilling out with a cool slap, when did they leave?

# 10

PACO'S BATTERY-POWERED ALARM clock went off a little after ten that night. I rubbed my eyes, rolled off the couch, and felt my pants and socks. They were dry, in fact, a little crackly to the touch—too much chlorine in that pool.

Within five minutes I was dressed and lacing my combat boots, all without a lamp. With the half-moon suspended in the sky, this time moving from full toward nothing, enough ambient shine slipped through the bay window. Didn't even have to use the flashlight.

I put on my knife, the pistol belt, and canteen and tied the .357 to a leather thong I'd slipped through the service belt, allowing the pistol to ride in a tight leather wrap that would unravel if I jerked the revolver by its grip. Hat in place and windbreaker half-zipped, I stepped out on the bunkhouse porch, making certain I didn't bang into anything. Noise discipline, man, I kept thinking, better get in the hang of it. There was a light on in the ranch house. Well, whoever was in there wouldn't see me, and they wouldn't hear me either, not even when I started the truck. After coming back to the bunkhouse, I'd gone and moved the truck behind the barn. Hay works wonders as a muffler, but I still clenched my teeth as the Chevy engine sprang to life. It didn't overstart or cough, it ran smooth, in tune, and I put it in low gear, easing across the field to the back road. No headlights please, and God forgive those tire-crunching noises and the sound of gravel reverberating against the fenders and steel frame.

A short half hour later I drove into the thicket below the ridge, well out of sight from anyone, anywhere. Back under a weedy arch of mesquite, maybe forty feet off the truck trail, I parked the pickup in backward, rolled up the windows, and left the key in the ignition. In another ten minutes I climbed over the Dickson fence line and onto Dickson land.

But this was my plan, wasn't it, though I still hadn't figured every last angle—something must be left to play by ear, something with balls and audacity. Maybe I really was going to kill Blaine. Him down in Harlingen—horseshit. He'd been horse racing on Sunday afternoon, and Monday morning he'd gunned down Paco, I knew that in my gut and felt it in my trigger finger. Then, well, maybe I wasn't going to kill Blaine. I wanted to get to the Dickson Ranch complex and look around—just for myself.

I'd spent some time perusing the aerial photograph, trying to line it up with my own mental picture of the terrain. A topo map would have been ideal—say, 1 to 25,000—but I had a good eyeball direction and a couple of definite reference points, the ridge for starters and a creek bed about a mile or so in. From there I planned to follow the draw or stay in the tree line and the scrub, just in case any stray cowboys with bazookas might be riding the plains. I felt good and moved quietly, with speed, and I remembered all the old aero-rifle platoon tricks—check the tree line for a flux of light, any shiny reflections, maybe a cigarette, look several places in succession, use the peripheral rods and cones in the old eyeballs and let the ones in the back, the ones that work better with less light, do their genetic thing.

Yet somehow I'd misfigured—it must have been more like two miles to the creek bed 'cause I stumbled in it just before midnight. Damn, I wasn't making very good time, maybe I was being too careful. I poured some water down my throat and moved on, sticking close to the creek's steep side and out of the moonlight.

A snort jumped out of a dark cranny, followed by a half-cocked squeal. Javelina. I took a dozen quick steps. The pigs stayed put, thank God—they can be mean and nasty when surprised.

I picked up the pace, trying to make better time.

About two o'clock I reached a bend I'd noticed in the photograph, one with a cascade of boulders and torn-down trees spreading across the bowed floodplain. If I was where I thought I was, I couldn't be but three miles as the crow flies from the headquarters of the Dickson Ranch, but that three could become a hard six down here on the ground. I lay against the steep side of the bend and caught my breath. Lessee. I'd have to lie low at dawn and see where everything went, where Blaine was staying, what moved and what didn't. What if Mr. Rawlins wasn't around? Well, I'd catch as catch could and give the Dicksons my best shot, so to speak.

Moonlight waned—good, I'd take a peek over the cliff, someplace where I could get a toehold and a handhold that wouldn't collapse into a pile of red dirt. About two hundred yards down the draw I found my spot and scrambled up the bank. I couldn't see anything except a thick line of mesquite. Well, that's cover, and I'd use it, making sure I didn't get silhouetted along the creek's embankment.

Three hundred yards later I stopped hard.

A yellow orange flame flared and lingered around a face with a cigarette clenched between its lips. The face took a long draw and sat down on a camp stool, a brush windbreak to his northside and a nice long shot up the creek to his south and west, a damn good position for a sentry. He wasn't but forty feet or so from me and I lay flat against the grit, the knob of a mesquite branch digging into my chest. Some kind of scoped carbine lay at his feet, no, better to say a carbine with some kind of king-size scope. He picked the rifle up, cradled it, then leaned it against his leg, and I saw it in silhouette—a Starlight scope in an automatic carbine mount—now that's a nice piece of equipment, and a nice piece of cash.

There was a break of radio squelch, I recognized the burst of electric sound. He picked up a hand mike and gave the button a squeeze. "Not a thing," he said. There was an answering crack of static.

I crawled beneath the mesquite, scraping hell out of my cheek on a prickly pear. What kind of crap had I gotten myself into, I thought, but then I knew I always thought that when I had to get around on my belly, snake like. Oh Christ. Now snakes and crawly beasts were things that could blow my soul away. I hoped all the rattlers and scorpions just stayed cool and out of my belly-down way.

The mesquite clump broke into an open space and a set of ruts. I stood up and almost banged into the Jeep parked beneath a thick turn of brush and gnarled wood. Skirting the jeep, I crossed the open space, then quietly moved into a grove of larger oak and palmetto.

Doggit—I hadn't considered facing anything fancy like Starlight scopes. Both sides in this whole hairy scene definitely traveled in large denominations. Yeah, I had a pill-size case of fear in my stomach. What if they were using dogs. I had only six goddamn rounds and I didn't want to waste them on Dobermans and bloodhounds, no sir.

From the break in the palmetto and mesquite thicket I

saw the faint lights of the ranch complex. I moved up to a barbed wire fence line, picked my way across it, and then worked back toward the jeep trail, almost breaking an ankle when I caught my boot in a grass-covered hole. I stopped. My watch said four thirty and I couldn't believe it, but the hazy blue gray of morning nautical twilight already gave a sharper form to the dark trees and I could see the certain edges of the distant buildings.

When I reached the wooden rail fence line, I knew where I was. Pulling the aerial photo out of my pocket, I took my jacket off and put it over my head as a light shield. Only then did I flip on the flashlight. Yeah, somewhere . . . here, along the gray line leading to the edge of the orange grease pencil. I looked at the "Hah!" and doused the light.

I was curious about the Hah, curious enough to investigate. Anyway, moving along the fence line gave me cover from the ranch, cover I might as well take advantage of since Dickson had so many well-armed eyeballs.

So move carefully, I told myself, take your time— you've got it—work along the fence line and the brush.

I hit the dirt as the doe leaped from the bushes, hooves clicking the top rail as it missed me and cleared the fence, a silvery brown side, then a white tail racing away. Jesus. The deer did a midair turn, gave the grass a glancing thump, and then sprang into the underbrush, disappearing.

Well, if I could sneak up on a deer, I must be doing something right, I concluded.

Using the fence as a reference point, I bypassed another thicket and worked through a field of stumps and cutting. The fence line took a bend, then ran another fifty yards and stopped in a tall nest of brown grass and weed. Gnarled mesquite posts, the ghosts of an older fence line, continued beyond the weeds. I crawled into the grass at the end of the rail fence and did some thinking. If I was going to get around the field to my left, not to mention the long plain of Hah leading to the ranch barns, I'd have to backtrack.

An engine started up, the familiar engine noise of copter beginning to crank and whine. There was now a lot of sunlight. Shoot, it was almost quarter to six. I stuck a blade of grass in my mouth and chewed on it. Might as well save the water a little longer. Might need it at noon.

The copter got its chops up to flight speed. Though it was out of direct sight, I had its location pinned, and there it rose, first a telltale flush of JP exhaust and then the spinning blades and the bird itself, a blue-and-white Jet Ranger, hovering, throwing grass like a rotary mower. That's when I heard the engine of the second ship, a deeper throat, a copter up in altitude.

The second craft's running lights were on, and I saw it moving in from the northeast, indirectly but then in a long parallel, as if it were tracing a road. Yeah, that's exactly what that bird's doing, I thought, it's flying a road.

The first chopper moved away from the stable area and jogged out into the middle of the wide grass field between me and the main ranch house, then it headed, still at ground-hugging height, toward the exit ranch road, popping up just in time to clear the telephone and power lines.

I got a better read on the second bird as it took a high turn to the west. Black-and-white, another Jet Ranger. The chopper turned, then took a fast dive toward the dirt. Whaaa? The blue-and-white helicopter went into a fast climb just as the black-and-white reached the treetops.

Radar switcheroo. One dives below air control sight, one immediately climbs to replace it, and the air controller, if he's even watching, thinks the first bird took a two-second dip.

The black-and-white chopper had "State Police—DPS" stenciled on its side. It landed beside the ranch house.

Yeah, I was curious as hell, double curious, and as long as the chopper was raising the local decibel level, I was going to take advantage of my chance. I slid back through the grass and dashed down along the old fence line, running beside the wireless posts. Yeah—the big field, the one circled in orange on the recon photo, did have some cover, as well as an outhouse-looking building stuck in the middle of it. I hadn't seen any structure in the photograph. I stopped and caught my breath. If I got across that field, I'd be within spitting distance of the stable area and the barns. From there I'd get my bearings and try to work my way up to the ranch house. I went down flat and took a minute's look.

I took another second to steady out, then stood up to a starting crouch.

"Freeze it right there, asshole!"

"He's covered."

I froze, arms straight up in the air.

"I knowed that wasn't some fuckin' deer." And I knew that voice was Blaine's.

"He's got a gun," the Mexican said. The man had a broad Indian face, bronze skin and a 9-millimeter Ingram submachine gun with MAC suppressor. He also had a very fine knife. With a deft slash he cut my .357 from its thong and tossed the gun at Blaine's feet.

"What'd I say to you, Sanchez?" Blaine yelled. "What'd I say?"

Sanchez sneered. "I said you should have dropped this nosy mother when you got Ramirez."

"Look at me, Buchanan," Blaine yelled. I did. He slammed his rifle's butt into my gut and I collapsed like a loose sack of shit. I think I heard a swarm of choppers take off and land. Blaine kicked my black hat back into the brush as Sanchez ripped off my pistol belt and knife. Then they both hog-tied my hands and ankles, stuffed an oily rag in my mouth, and tossed me in the back of a Jeep truck that drove across the field. I caught a nice boot in the side and part of a heel in the head and the sun beat my eyes shut as I lay there, Blaine ranting, ordering some other joker to go catch his horse.

They didn't watch the bumps going back to the ranch either. I felt a trickle of salty blood mixing with the oil rag and I started to throw up but held it down. If I couldn't push the gag out when I chucked, then I'd drown in my own vomit—good God, what a silly-ass way to die.

"Naw, fuckit, make him walk."

Sanchez cut the bind around my ankles and pulled the gag out of my mouth. I coughed and threw up.

"Better not splatter on my tires," Sanchez said, giving me a kick in the butt.

I got a look at Blaine and the rifle he carried, a carbine now lazily pointing toward the ground—yes, a thirty-thirty saddle gun, octagonal barrel. Well, Sanchez had said Blaine'd shot Paco. "That the rifle you used, Blaine?" I asked.

"C'mon," he muttered, now pointing the barrel at me and then swinging it toward the rear of the ranch house. Some house, too. Three stories, hard yellow paint, set in a grove of tall, wide live oak, trees with thick trunks winding like constrictors in the air. "Move it, Buchanan." I moved it, through the backyard and up a short wooden stoop, through the kitchen and into a long hall. "Take a hard right," Blaine barked.

A old man hunched over the pool table, lining up a shot. It was Dickson. "Holt a second," he muttered. Over the fireplace mantel a long pair of cattle horns spread like a white smile, a lamp with a stained-glass shade sat on the dark wood desk. The cue stick moved. "Combination, right corner," the old man said, touching his long gray mustache. The combination missed and the cue ball dropped into a side pocket.

"Tough scratch," Blaine said.

"Especially before breakfast." Dickson cleared his throat. "This the other fella?"

"Yeah," Blaine replied.

Dickson coughed and cleared his throat again. He wore a hand-stitched white shirt with silver trim, a pair of jeans, and a pair of hand-tooled boots. "What should we do with him?" he said.

"You asking me?" Blaine replied, sounding surprised. The old man nodded. "Shit. Shoot the mother."

"I don't want to hear about it," Dickson said, returning to the table.

"Well, then you candyass won't, Mr. Dickson. C'mon," Blaine told me, giving me a punch with the rifle barrel.

"Hey, Blaine," Dickson said, retrieving the cue ball and setting the table again, intending to reshoot the missed combination. "Now holt on, Blaine—what's this fella know?"

"He's a liar."

"I ain't asking what he is, I'm asking what he knows."

"I knowed he saw Colonel Harrison land."

The old man blanched. "You got a dumb mouth, cowboy—now I guess you will have to kill him."

Blaine looked confused. "Didn't you just tell me to shoot him anyway?"

"You *know* how I feel about shooting lawmen, especially federal agents." The old man lined up the cue stick and the white ball.

"Hey, thought you'd told me that Harrison said Buchanan's a nobody."

Who, me? I thought. A nobody? Well, Harrison was just about right, it seemed.

Dickson nodded. "Yeah, I say a lot of things. And now

I'm sayin' what if Harrison's wrong?" Dickson punctuated his last sentence with a poke of the pool cue.

"He better not be too wrong," Blaine said coldly.

"Well, what if he is . . . what if he's caught short on a lot of things? Why, we might be, to say the least, in a heap of pain."

"You want me to beat on him 'til he talks?"

"I want you to work on *your* priorities. There's a lot goin' down now. We'll let Freddy talk to, ah, Mr. Buchanan."

"Carrizo's comin' here?"

"This afternoon."

"What the hell for?" Blaine turned and looked at me. Dickson didn't answer. Blaine set the saddle gun's octagonal barrel against my temple. "Heck, Freddy'll just cut this guy to pieces. Freddy uses a diamond razor, motherfucker," Blaine said to me. "God, I knew you were police when I first laid eyes on you."

"Now don't jump to any conclusions. Just look at, ah, Mr. ah . . ."

"You just called me Buchanan," I said.

Dickson smiled. "Consider Mr. Buchanan as a potential insurance policy."

"God, I knowed he was police no matter what Harrison says." Blaine shook his head angrily.

"Now you do your business and get Sanchez to find a cooler for this ugly man," Dickson said, pointing the cue at me. "Then, we'll let Fast Freddy speak with him." Dickson rocked back on his bootheels, lined up the cue ball, and made the shot. Bang bang bang, right corner pocket, the number three ball drops. "It worked," Dickson said, grinning.

"Anything else, Mr. Dickson?" Blaine asked.

Dickson waved his hand and went to his desk. "If there is, I don't want to hear about it."

And I didn't want to hear about it either, but I did, and I

felt it, too. Blaine butt-kicked me down the back stoop. "Goddamn, I knowed you was a cop."

We walked underneath the huge twisted oaks. "What'd you think your stupid ass was gonna find here *this* mornin'?"

I looked back at him. "You'd never believe me if I told you."

He punched me and I slammed against oak bark. "Try me."

I grinned. "I's comin' over here to take you up on that job you wanted to gimme."

He slapped my face and broke open my upper lip. "Try me again."

"Blaine—I'm not a cop."

His browless eyes knit together. Whap, a slap from the other side. "I'm not stupid," he said. "Hey, Sanchez!"

Sanchez walked up the driveway, the submachine gun swinging at his side. "Yeah?"

"Put this dude somewhere."

"Kill him?"

Blaine said no, wait. "Dickson wants Carrizo to talk to him."

Sanchez winced at Carrizo's name. "Where'll I take him? The back house maybe?"

Blaine said the back house was fine. He gave me one last look and walked off toward a couple of pickups parked down the drive.

The back house was a fancy two-story building, Victorian scroll work, open porch, the same hard yellow color—it was the building attached to the main house by a long covered walkway that I'd seen in the recon photo. Sanchez said to walk, slamming his palm in the middle of my back every so often—to make sure I heard him, he gave as his reason. Hands still tied behind my back, I waited by the porch swing while he fiddled with the screen door. He finally kicked it open and pushed me through, the door swinging back and hitting him in the head. He cursed in Spanish, then told me to walk up the hall. I did. We went upstairs into a small back room with a single bed stuck in the corner.

The room was hot and stuffy. "Dammit," Sanchez said. "Well, sit down on the bed." He made sure I sat before he opened the window. "Dammit," he yelled again. "Hey, bring me a fan." Then he said something in Spanish about water. "You here?" he called through the door and into the hall. There was no reply. "Don't think I'm gonna baby-sit with you all day, motherfucker," Sanchez said, wiping his brow. He wore a brown T-shirt and he'd sweat through the cotton in large splotches.

I closed my eyes, then opened them. Sanchez was lighting a cigarillo, blowing the smoke out the window.

"Madre," he yelled, "did you hear me?"

Madre? I remembered the old woman with the gray-black hair. This could get interesting, I thought, if only it weren't cut short—it being my life.

Sanchez smoked for about five minutes, looking quickly through the window, then back at me. Finally he stuck the cigarillo bit between his teeth and lay back in the rocking chair, his hands behind his head. "You really an FBI agent?" he asked. I said no, and it hurt like hell to say anything with my lip swelling so. "Drug Enforcement then?" I said no again. "Fine, fine," Sanchez said. He glanced out the window. "Hey, muchacho," he yelled, then whistled. "Hey, up here. Can you get me a string of rope?" He opened the shutter a little more and leaned out. I started to sit up. "Two pieces yay long," he said, spreading his arms. He popped back in the room. "That's right, motherfucker, you think smart and I pop you with this," he patted the Ingram," and then I don't waste a morning sitting on my ass."

Ten minutes later another man, an Anglo in a powder blue shirt, showed up with a ball of twine. "Okay, that'll have to do," Sanchez said. The cowboy left as Sanchez drew his knife and cut off a couple of long strands. "Down on the floor," he ordered. I got down. He tied my ankles together, then ran a piece of twine from the ankle tie to the wrist tie, hobbling me nice and tight. "Get back on the bed." I fell flat the first time I tried. Sanchez laughed. I made it the second time. "I'm going up the hall," he said. He started to leave, then he stopped. "No, I ain't just yet." He cut another piece of twine, made a loop out of it, and put the loop around my neck. He tied the other end to the bed post. "Now I won't have to worry. You can drag the bed and choke for all I care."

I lay in the bed, trying to figure out an angle. All I got was a wide plain of nothing, no intersections, just a straight stretch run to the graveyard or a hungry buzzard's gut. I sneezed a couple of times and tried to work on the rope around my wrists. Though my arms were gong to sleep, I could still move my hands a little, just a little, which was the sign of a professional tie job. Enough movement to keep the blood flowing, but not enough room for the victim to move a dime with.

He came back a half hour or so later, holding a glass of ice water. He muttered something to himself in Spanish— I couldn't pick it out—and he sat down. For two hours he gave the world a bored expression, staring out the window, watching the morning change. He left and then returned, I asked him if I could take a leak, he thought a second, said why not, then cut my neck loose and the tie between my ankles and wrists. We went down the hall, me jumping.

"I ain't unzipping you," he said.

"I ain't asking you to. So cut'em." He cut my wrist ties and I used the john. Back in the room he started to tie me up again. "Hey, lemme keep my hands in front, okay? My arms keep going to sleep." He thought about it for a moment, then said all right.

Sanchez gave the Ingram a pat. "You won't run anywhere anyway . . . I guess you can be a little comfortable. You at least keep your mouth shut."

I took off my windbreaker and tossed it on the floor. Sanchez tied my hands in front of me, attached a new ankle tie, then sat down in his chair and smoked another cigarillo. I lay back on the bed. The mattress felt like a dump—hell, it smelled like a dump, a dump of old sweat-soaked rags.

We both heard a door open and slam downstairs. "Hey," Sanchez shouted. "Madre? Dese prisa!" He yelled something else about being thirsty and hungry. "Arriba," he said.

There was no answer. Then she came through the door, a wall of quietness in a blue shawl. "What did you say, Arturo?"

He relit the cigarillo and repeated what he'd said, this time not shouting, sounding almost respectful.

She glanced at me. "Como esta?" she asked.

"Estoy perdido."

Sanchez snickered. "I'm going to perdido your head, puerco." He raised his boot and put a nasty toe job to my leg. "Comprende that. Huh?"

I must have winced. I understood the pain as I licked at my lips. "I'll bring him something, too," Madre said as she left.

Looking for an opening, I asked Sanchez who the old woman was and he shrugged. "An old lady. Worked here 'fore Dickson bought this place. Why?"

I said I didn't know. "Just curious, looking for some way to pass the time."

Sanchez snickered again and pointed his submachine

gun at me. "Won't have to wait much longer, cop man."
He laughed and looked around for someplace to spit. He
spit on the floor.

Madre returned, carrying a tray. "Cut the tie," she told
Sanchez, meaning the bind between my wrists and
ankles. He gave her a suspicious look but pulled out his
knife and sliced it. "Sit up," she said to me. My hands
latched on to the glass of ice water and I downed it.

There was a bottle of mescal on the tray—one could see
the dead grub sunk at the bottom—along with a pair of
glasses, one half-filled with water and the other with ice.

Sanchez let out a low whistle when he saw the mescal.
"Bueno," he said. "Uh, how come?"

Madre said, roughly—I didn't get all the Spanish—why
not, but he shouldn't drink too much. Sanchez nodded
and poured a finger's worth over the ice. "Just a shot,
friend," he said to me, "any more and I'd get into trouble.
Thanks, old woman," he said to Madre. He poured himself another couple of fingers. "Hey, Madre," he grinned,
offering her the mescal, "you better take the bottle, eh?
Maybe I can't control myself." She took the bottle.

"I'll bring you a sandwich," she said to Sanchez. He
nodded and took a sip of water, then an equal-size sip of
iced mescal.

"Don't you drink that stuff with salt and lime?" I asked.

"I just drink this stuff," he said, deciding to kick the
whole drink back.

I put my head flat on the bed and stared at the ceiling.
Sanchez glanced out the window, took the clip off his sub,
fiddled with it, then slammed it back into position. "Hell,"
he said, "forgot to tell that old bitch to bring me a fan." He
stood up. "Madre . . ." he started to yell. His knees wob-
bled and his face lightened two shades of pink.

Hot damn, I thought, she'd done it.

"No," he rasped. He managed to turn and point the Ingram at me. "Don't think . . .' bout trying."

I kicked my bound legs up, and the submachine gun went flying. Sanchez slipped and grabbed for the gun. I bounced off the mattress and brought my boots down hard on his jaw. There was a sharp, then a brittle mashing sound. He had his hand on the sub and then he didn't.

Madre was at the door. She bent down over Sanchez, calling him Arturo, then she pulled a feather out of her hair and held it to his nose. "Good, he's still alive," she said, looking down at me as I sat on the floor. "Well?" she asked.

"Well what? Can you let me loose?"

"Did you have to break his jaw?"

"Can I help it if he falls 'cause he can't hold his liquor?"

She smiled and said something in Spanish.

I shook my head. "I can't understand it that fast," I said.

"Buchanan, I said you have a deadman's humor." She picked up Sanchez's long knife and cut my wrists free. I took the knife and undid my ankles.

"What am I supposed to do now?" I asked her.

"It looks to me like you are free and you have a gun."

"Uh, yeah. What more could I ask?"

Her black eyes looked through my eyes and rattled around in my skull. "You aren't a policeman, are you?"

"No ma'am," I said.

She sighed. "And Paco was, wasn't he?"

"I don't know, but it sure seems like it."

She sighed again. "I know he was. Of my grandsons, the very best. I am so sorry he died . . . heartbroken."

I looked at her. There were no tears in her eyes, but I felt the sap of at least two in mine—I won't deny it. But her face remained firm, like a full leather muscle whose deep lines wouldn't even quiver.

"I'm sorry, too."

"He gave you a job."

"Yeah, when I was feeling pretty desperate."

"And Blaine killed him?" she asked.

I said yeah. "I think so—Sanchez said Blaine did it."

I've seen dark looks pass over a face, but then I saw a deep darkness come to her face, a look from the freeze of heart-cold blood. "Arturo told you that?" she asked, listening to herself, knowing full well I'd simply repeat what I'd said. "Stupid liar!" she spit. She grabbed his knife from my hand, yanked him by the hair, and in one quick motion cut his throat.

"Goddamn."

A gush of blood spilled across the rug. "They'll think you did it," she said calmly, slipping the knife into a pocket of her dress.

"But . . . why for chrissakes!?"

"Don't stammer boy. And why act like a coward?"

"Bu . . ."

She looked down and through me, and I quit stammering. "Just kill Blaine like you kill a sick dog and you will owe me nothing."

"Whatever . . ." I managed.

"Don't try to go back across that . . . that runway. More planes are coming in tonight and they've got dogs and men out there. They know the police are around. Kill Blaine, then get out, that way," she said, pointing to the west. "There is a draw on the far side of the big corral. Follow it to the rocks and from there to the highway. Then run a very long way, eh?"

"Should I get the police?"

She laughed. "The police? They'll be here anyway," she said cynically.

I picked up the Ingram and checked the safety. Nice, light, and it throws a lot of lead. "Where's Blaine now?" I asked.

"I think he is over at Dickson's airplane. It's inside the far barn."

I thought about the Piper Cub in the alley between the stables. "I think I know where that is."

"You go," she nodded. "I will find this mess in an hour or two."

I closed the catch on the sub. "One thing, Madre. Do you know of a Freddy Carrizo?"

"The boy?"

"I don't think so. Blaine talks like Carrizo's a big honcho."

She shook her head from side to side. "He is a man I do not know," she said coldly.

I gave her a peck on the cheek 'cause I didn't have the guts to give her a bigger one.

"Vamoose," she whispered.

I didn't look at Sanchez.

I moved down the hall, made sure the porch was clear and that no one was in the backyard, and I went out the kitchen door. I had to calm myself, to tell myself to slow down and move natural like, easy in the joints, and not go flying pell-mell through the oak grove and to the stables, ready to blaze at anything that breathed.

I crossed the back road and reached the first barn, a one-story job with white metal siding. A high wooden fence ran from the back of the barn toward a big corral, where a tall black stallion, a well-muscled thoroughbred, poked its head between the white slats, trying to nibble on a sunflower. I went to the fence. There were two corrals, one empty and small—it stood between me and the stallion—then the large one that wasn't a corral at all but a huge field with thick green grass. I hopped the fence and crossed the small corral, figuring on getting around a couple of stables and back toward the one where I thought Blaine might be, if he was working on Dickson's plane, and, of course, if that's where the aircraft was parked.

I straddled the far fence and dropped softly to the dry muck earth. The cowboy in the powder blue shirt walked out of a stall, leading a quarter horse.

"Hey," he yelled, and I saw a hand move toward the holstered six-gun at his waist. I let the Ingram loose and with one fast brat—a sharp crack that still pierced the MAC suppressor on its barrel—his body split in half and the quarter horse reared and shot down the alley between the two horse barns. I dashed the other way, over the fence, through the corral, and into the field with the thoroughbred. The big stallion shied away, then took off to the far corner of the field, stretching out like a graceful black spring. Christ—I couldn't have ridden that thing anyway, I thought, hustling for every step I could get, the sub banging against my thigh and hip.

Thwack. Whoever fired was wild and high and the slope of the grassland gave me a gravity boost as well as dropped me out of line of sight.

I heard a couple of shots and just kept the legs pumping.

Thwack. Another round but no buzz from a near hit. I reached the far fence line, grabbed the top rail and heaved, half expecting a rifle round to slam into my back.

Nothing doing. I landed on the other side. There was a trail leading off toward the draw and I followed it, clutching the sub with both hands.

Oh shit.

The magazine had banged loose. No ammo. I looked around my feet. No dice. The clip must have come loose while pounding across the field. Why, for chrissakes? What a candyass piece of garbage. Well, I wasn't going back to try to find it. I threw the gun at the ground and ran up the draw.

# 11

THE BLUE-AND-WHITE Jet Ranger kept buzzing off to the north between the long rock ridge and the highway, working a search pattern. Damn my luck—they thought I was worth coming after.

I lay on a bed of flint and gravel between two rocks, a yucca plant and palmetto fronds shading my head. Having done my time in scout helicopters, I knew what they could and couldn't see, and I knew they could see a lot. I bent my body into the half L-shape that, from the air, is so tough to call human. A good trick, lie on the side, bend from the waist at a forty-five-degree angle, and hold it. This shadow isn't one that's easily read as a normal human shadow, and for the good aero scout, judging shadows is one of the trade's big tricks. I grinned and tore a long strip off my shirt and ragged it around my forehead. In all likelihood they didn't have anybody in that bird with eyes trained like mine. Still, as long as the aircraft moved in that search path, I'd have to lay low or go the other way. Did I mind?

I'd just about decided to save the old skin and forget Blaine. I'd head off to the south into salt lake country, then get the hell out. Just leave Blaine, Dickson, and the whole rowdy bunch—and Carrizo for that matter—for the cops.

I picked my way up a gully and cleared a crest, working back through the brush and prickly pear. Yeah, I was tired of this lowlife shit, avoiding cacti and thorn branches, and I was working on a heavy thirst.

The chopper moved off to the south. I heard its engines change pitch. Coming down? Well, I'd use the time. If they were setting down a rifleman like the Air Cav, outflanking me on the ground, that would complicate things. I figured on them running a Jeep or two along the highway, but if I had to move as if every bend were a potential ambush, well, I might as well not move at all. Damn—if there were so many cops in this thing, where were they when the public needed them? I felt like a very lonely public.

Then my brain, slow and methodical like it is, placed Harrison—as Harrison in lieutenant colonel, state cops. Yeah, I'm sort of slow on some things, but when your head's been kicked in by a double-barreled set of boots, sometimes the nerves don't fire at an Ivy League rate. And did I have a good headache, ornery, bull ugly.

Lt.C. Harrison—so they had them a big-size cop. Maybe I was better off on my own.

I stepped on a red scorpion, crushed it, and just kept moving.

The draw intersected a cut running north-south and I took the south fork. It bent farther to the west, across a salty wash and toward a clump of mesquite and chinery. The chopper's whump whump whump returned, somewhere north of me, if I wasn't getting an echo. I've watched guys on the ground looking the other way, sure I was coming at them from the far tree line, so sure that those NVA had their .51s set to turn me into a flaming ball of roasted meat, and then, of course, here I come from the back of the mind, mini-gun revved and spitting the gospel of American lead.

But now I was getting a good look at the ground pounders' point of view, and I didn't like what I saw and felt.

I jogged across the wash and rested under a mesquite branch. Face it, Billy, I thought, yeah, face it all, kid, this ain't the way to run your business.

I knew I was just buying time. Either they'd shoot me and drag off my carcass or the snakes and coyotes and buzzards would get a dehydrated meal. New issue, one man's body, dehydrated, no water, just add fangs.

I shook that off and clambered up the rock ledge.

Near the top I ducked under a twisted dead tree, and my boots started to slip in the gritty sand. I grabbed the branch, it broke and I rolled down the gully, banging my ribs and legs.

I started laughing. Who'd have thought it? I laughed again. I was better off in Saint Louis, cursing the government and pleading with the Salvation Army.

My whole head felt hot. I kept laughing.

Wasn't Detroit a stone-cold crashing bore? I said.

I might have yelled it.

My whole head felt like fire.

No. I caught my tongue. God, I'd have to get some water or go stark-blazing mad. I ran down the draw toward the south.

The chopper sounded very near, then the noise faded. I fell down on my knees. Could a man drink a prickly pear? I felt the inside of my mouth with my tongue. There was still moisture, I wasn't that thirsty, there was no reason to be crazy. I plucked one of the large, lobe-like cactus fronds and pulled off a half-dozen needles, then broke the frond in two. There was a greenish mulch inside, it tasted bitter and there wasn't much moisture. I spit the sourness out. Okay, get on with it. Two small pebbles lay at my feet. I dusted them off and put them in my mouth. Two sucking stones, well, I'd swallow my own saliva for a while, until I got toward the road and ambushed me a Jeep.

In another half hour I'd worked my way south of the ridgeline, the chopper nowhere in sight or in sound. West, that's where I figured I should go.

Then the ridge turned in front of me and cut back toward the south. I did some dead reckoning. West over that ridge I'd be able to see the road, either that or I'd find I was good and lost.

I looked to my left. The dazzling haze of a reflective salt lake spun in the distance. Better that it be a mirage than undrinkable, bitter water?

I heard the helicopter coming, from the north.

Well, over the rise.

I checked, didn't see anything, then rolled over the ridgetop, clambering down through the mesquite.

A rooster tail of dust, led by a blue Jeep, spewed off a dirt trail that ran out of a gully, a gully I figured led to the highway.

I went into a controlled fall, sliding down the steep dirt side, then cutting back into a line of rock and weed just as the first rifle bullet whined over my head. The second shattered in the rocks, kicking white fragments out like broken teeth.

The next round zipped high, knocking somewhere into the red clay cliff, and I kept scrambling, using all fours, a survival animal looking for a hole.

The gray pig let out a death scream as it leaped from the brush in front of me, taking the rifle round in its belly. Squealing and bleeding, the javelina tore along the base of the cliff, me following the wounded animal, the mesquite trees suddenly giving us both a little concealment. The pig stumbled to the left, then ran off through the underbrush.

I heard the chopper and took to the right, digging up a cleft in the ridge.

Box canyon, no, end of the draw, with a break where I could see, through the high brush, a cowboy with white hat knocking his way through the thick mesquite.

To the right was a little cliff and I pulled myself up on it, into the shade, trying to worm my way onto the ridge itself.

That pig—I cursed it. This morning a deer and now a slimy wild pig. Animals had it in for this Buchanan, to say nothing of a posse's worth of human cobras.

And the joke was on me, wasn't it? I should have been saying rattlers—a rattler, as in big and diamondback, flopping down on my leg. I caught the snake behind its head, its jaws unhinging, its tail slamming like a gator in water, strong and hard, the shaker vibrating like BB's in a deadly gourd. Using my other hand, I grabbed the rattlesnake midway down its four-foot body and it fought me, whipping its muscles hard, flopping against me and the little cliff.

The chopper flew down the ridgeline and passed overhead. I rolled so that the snake was pinned between me and the ridge and I looked into its hard, hate-filled eyes.

The damn snake was as scared of me as I was of it.

Yeah, the rattler had its poison, behind its hiss, in those curving fangs, but I had the viper's neck in an unbreakable choke hold, ready to snap its pitted head with one sure twist.

"Blood heah!"

Somebody was shouting from below the draw.

And there was Bennet, his head three-quarters turned away, his white hat kicked back, the pouches of his sagging face quivering with a volatile mix of fear and excitement and fatigue.

"Wheah?" he yelled. "He couldn't have gotten down there." Bennet turned away from me and took two steps up the gully, then saw that it boxed out and ended in a mud gray-and-red side.

The VC used to stick kraits in the roofs of tunnels. Whap—one snake-bit GI and death from a living booby trap. Well, I wouldn't have to use that, Blaine had about had enough of this chase business it seemed. He was ready to follow the trail of that gut-shot pig and certify it as a human kill.

I watched his back relax and his arms bring the rifle down. Right on ole Bennet, 'member there's a cold one back at the ranch. A cold one—I licked my lips and thought about how good a brew would taste.

And an involuntary cough I couldn't stifle broke from my throat. I threw the snake in Bennet's general direction and came down after it.

Bennet spun toward me, but I didn't hit him—the crazy rattler did, like a loose coil of moving rope, its jaws catching on to Bennet's lower neck and the fangs sinking in.

Bennet screamed and grabbed for the snake, his left arm losing the rifle and the rifle bouncing down the slope. I took two quick steps and leaped to the right, sliding down the break beneath the low limbs of a mesquite, then rolling hard into the red earth. Bennet fell about twenty feet away, and God know's where the snake crawled to.

A tall Mexican scrambled up to Bennet. "Hay-sus!" he yelled, then he started screaming in fast Spanish.

"What is it?"

"Bennet. Hit by a snake."

"Bad, real bad." Another cowboy was bending over Bennet.

"You gone suck it out, Marshall?"

Marshall was already doing a vampire bit on Bennet's neck. "There's a kit in the chopper. Call the chopper and get him to a hospital."

The big vaquero raced down the hill. I slid quietly backward, inching my own way down the slope, keeping the brush between me and Bennet, and the gully wall between me and where the chopper had landed.

At the bottom of the draw I peered around the edge of the cut. The Jet Ranger's rotor made slow arcs, and the tall Mexican and one of the pilots were already running back up the hill.

To the right, about three hundred yards away, another man was hunkering down, examining something. Javelina blood? I didn't see the Jeep. Good gosh, was I ever outmanned!

"I'm gonna carry him down," Marshall yelled.

"Movin' him just makes the poison faster," someone yelled back.

"He's goddamn near dead anyway."

I couldn't see what was going on. Five minutes later Marshall and his crowd were down by the chopper, working on Bennet's body. The pilot started to rev the engine one more time.

So I stayed put, moving about six feet deeper into the mesquite and sitting down. I had a good shot at getting out of this thing, something I hadn't expected. I slapped at a gnat, and the chopper's engine reached takeoff speed. In this heat starting and stopping an engine like that ran the risk of a burnout, not a big risk, but still a betting proposition. But, naw, that wasn't my worry, was it? No telling how much poison that snake had pumped and how much time Bennet had. The snake wasn't ready to strike and it was off balance when it hit him. Maybe Bennet would pull through, depending on how close those fangs were to his juggler. Maybe he'd had a heart attack. I felt my own neck, then checked around the area. A man couldn't count on being faster than a snake more than once a day.

The tall chicano cowboy was walking back up the ridge-line. "Hey, Smitty," he yelled. "Get your ass back here."

The Mexican stood there, a Remington .308 in his right hand. A couple of minutes later the man I'd seen down the ridge arrived. I heard the chopper lift off and fly away, in the direction of the road.

Smitty was breathing hard.

"Well, what do you think?" the tall vaquero asked.

"I dunno, Purdy. We sure saw a man running up this line. But that sucker must have an awful lot of blood."

"You check the spring?"

"Up toward it," Smitty replied, jerking his head.

"Gimme a drink from your canteen," Purdy told him. Smitty gave the tall man his canteen and the Mexican let it flood his mouth and spill. I swallowed and got only dryness. And the dice rattle of two saliva stones heard only in my head.

"What do you think, strawboss?" Smitty asked.

"I think it looks like a gut-shot javelina."

Smitty nodded. "Could be. But we both saw a man."

"Yeah, I know. Well, I think Bennet's gonna die."

"From a snakebite?"

The Mexican touched his neck. "Right here. The man was already cold."

"So what does he want us to do?"

"Marshall thinks we shot ourselves an FBI agent, but he don't know nothin' about hunting. He saw all that blood on those first rocks and told me a man couldn't move more than a hundred yards after being hit like that. That's bullshit—Marshall don't know."

"So what are we gonna do?" Smitty asked again.

"You're gonna follow me to the Jeep and we're gonna get the hell out of here."

They moved down the ridge and then out of sight behind a stand of oak and dead brush. I started back up the ridgeline, toward the east, back toward the ranch. Dryness. Goddamn, I still had those awful pebbles beneath my tongue. Lot of good they'd done me. I plucked them out of my mouth and dropped them in the sand.

Three hundred yards down the line I saw a flush of green, soft nonwaxy green, a grove of half-size oaks that, though they were twisted and stunted, looked wet to the touch. The line of green brush ran for a couple hundred yards, then it too trickled off, dropping into a gulch that yawned of dryness.

No matter. I found the spring. The water tasted cool, it tasted fresh, and, though the liquid left a brackish sting and in the hollow of the spring nested yellow-bodied spiders, so close my lips caught a trace of web, I gulped down handful after splashing handful.

# 12

I DECIDED TO TAKE one last crack at Blaine.

Madre. I owed her. I owed myself. And I'm not the kind of guy who calls it even when it isn't.

Three hours later, a little before seven—I checked my watch for the first time in an eon or so—I reached the draw below the stallion's field and crept through the high brush, looking for that busted Ingram. Someone had scarfed up the sub. Well, I wouldn't have found the clip anyway.

Lying down in the grass, I peered through the rail fence, wondering where the guards were. The dry bermuda brought on an itch. Guards? My answer came across the stallion's field on horseback, over the rise beyond the oaks, two men on Appaloosas, carbines up. They brought their mounts to a fast trot, then rode hard toward the far side of the meadow, stopping at a double gate.

If I stayed low, they couldn't see me. Slipping under the fence I ran toward the tall oak grove, back bent, trying to keep an arc of the slope between me and the riders. They were just beyond that far gate and slowly remounting when I disappeared among the trees.

Further up the grove, beneath a thin pecan, the black stallion grazed quietly. Two mares, one fat with foal, stood by a brick of yellow salt. I walked among the horses. The mares whinnied softly, then began to lick the block. I looked back for the riders and saw no sign of them. Sunset reddened the horizon. A breeze picked up, a new wind that beneath the shading trees felt almost cool.

So the grove ran west to east. If I followed it to the end, I figured on coming out behind two big barns, both of them a good half mile south of the ranch house. I lay down on a thick mat of goat grass, got the air recon photo out of my wallet—that dummy Blaine had been too busy busting my face to take my wallet—and located the barns. Of all the Dickson Ranch buildings they were the farthest out and the farthest south. Four hundred yards to their north the stable area began, a group of six one-story structures built parallel like a bunch of parked rectangles. I'd shot the man in the powder blue shirt in the space between the top two, smack dab in the middle of the airplane in the photo. But there hadn't been a plane there this morning. That puzzled me. Madre had mentioned Dickson's airplane—had she meant the blue-and-white helicopter? Who knew what that woman meant? And where was the copter now, still off at the hospital?

My brain quit worrying about aircraft when I remembered Madre's warning about dogs. I got a fresh case of goosebumps—this time there wasn't a .357 Magnum dog killer at my side. So quit screwing around, huh Buchanan? I looked at the two barns in the photo. The plain of Hah lay just to the east of the buildings. Well, the grove led there anyway, may as well go with the ground cover.

I moved carefully, staying low until the trees stopped

about forty yards from the fence line and the back of the barns, two huge white metal forms. The north barn had an aeromotor electrical generator on the rear of its roof, its gray blade revolving slowly in the light northwestern wind. I took a deep breath, walked quickly across the field, and slid beneath the fence. Hustling into the wide alley between the two barns, I frightened a couple of chickens and nearly stepped on a tired, fragile-looking bloodhound. The sad dog didn't even bother to bark. Okay, fella, I said, easy. He sniffed my palm. The barn with the aeromotor had two side doors, and I stepped into the nearest entrance, then crouched behind a bale of hay. It didn't take long for my pupils to adjust to the darkness. I listened—no movement, the only sound my own breath. There was another door along the far wall, just past the big object I recognized as a twin-engine Beech King Air. A rim of light ran around the sides and across the bottom of the front end of the barn—yes, a hangar door. And the whole building smelled of hay and aviation fuel. My pilot's nostrils twitched—such a nasty combination.

I jumped out of my gourd when the bloodhound poked his nose through the door and gave my hand a friendly lick. Dammit, boy, I whispered, scratching his head, don't do that to your friends, huh, fella? As the hound wandered back outside, I noticed a bank of light switches to the left of the door. Well, since I don't think anyone's home, let's shed some light on the subject. I flipped on one of the switches, then quickly shut it off. No response. Good, nobody's rolling in the hay.

I turned the light back on. The single bulb hung above a huge machine, a massive air compressor. One wide intake hose ran up the rear wall and connected to a gasket in the roof. Three smaller lines, each one about the size of a hefty garden hose, ran from the compressor toward the hangar door, bending underground at a metal socket just inside the building.

Leaving the bulb on, I walked over to the airplane. The blue King Air, a pair of white stripes along its side, had no civilian ID numbers. I put my hand on the craft's cold metal nose, then checked the cabin door—shut tight, tight as a drum.

A couple of empty av gas barrels lay under the plane's tail. Another barrel sat on a metal dolly beneath a pair of pulleys and a steel pipe frame. They gassed the craft by gravity feed—get a nozzle, raise the barrel in the frame, and let it flow. I gave the barrel in the dolly a thump. Thud. It was full.

I found a beat-up Huck Finn–style straw hat sitting on a stack of five-gallon gasoline cans. By the far wall, on top of a wrap of air hose, lay a rake and a denim jacket. My torn shirt wouldn't cut it if the night got cool. I put the jacket on and picked up the rake, then got the hat, tilting it over my brow. The somewhat peon look just might work as a disguise, I thought, especially from a distance.

Over by the compressor I picked up a foot-long piece of three-quarter-inch pipe and slipped it into my jacket pocket, then I went back to the switch, flipped off the light and returned to the north door. Okay, let's get some bearings. There were the stables, four hundred yards away. Waiting here by the plane seemed like the easiest option, but was it the best? I looked east to the plain of Hah. Yeah, there was that funny-looking wreck of a building with sagging sides, the one that didn't appear in the recon photo. I pulled my wallet out and looked at the worn photo fragments one more time. As an airfield, the scene just didn't make sense. You just couldn't begin to land a plane in that field unless it were some kind of special VSTOL model—Very Short Takeoff and Landing. Hell, in this case the V should stand for "vertical." I shook my head. Naw, those big stumps were problem enough. A Piper Cub might just squeeze it out, but a King Air was, in comparison, a runway-eating behemoth. How in the hell would you land a B-25 out there unless you were staging a crash? Mexican kamikazes? I snickered. Kamikazes left litter, lots of wreckage to dispose of and lots of fires to snuff out. No, I was missing something.

I wandered back to the King Air, carrying the rake on my shoulder. Beneath the light switches by the far door the bloodhound curled up in the hay, snoozing. I went over and gave the dog another scratch behind the ears. You like me ole pup? He gave a pleasant moan and rolled over. Some guard dog—I was glad to see that everything on this ranch didn't have a large streak of mean.

A streak of mean. The act—Madre slashing Sanchez— flashed through my mind. I tried to shunt it into some side cavity, into a dark and forgettable spot in the skull. Who could know what went on in her brain? One minute damning me for cracking the sucker's jaw, the next second cutting through his throat with about as much emotion as some people have when they skewer pigs. Villa's lover—I believed it, maybe she'd poisoned him, after balling the guy in the back of a cantina.

The bloodhound got up and walked across the alley and did his thing against the other barn. And I decided I didn't like staying put. If I could get to the back house and find Madre, the odds were good she'd have a gun. She sure as hell had a knife.

The sun was almost sunk, its rays red and gold. Good, with the straw hat and denim jacket, walking slowly while dragging a rake, I'd be someone else in the graying twilight. Better get to those stables. But how to get to the back house and old Madre? Hiding in the night was like yelling shoot me, if these boys brought out the Starlight scopes, but then the ranch house lights stayed on at night and ambient light devices wash out when there's too much shine. Damn—all these razored mental angles, they were enough to slice your mind.

So the hell with it. I walked down the alley, checked my left and took a right along the fence, walking behind the barn, beyond the barn toward the stables, the rake on my shoulder. Okay, I said, let's be cool and methodical. Nobody's in sight, nothing's moving, only the thoroughbred and his mares, no one behind me, no one in front, then a car door slamming and I swallow my jaw but hell, the car's a long way away, up by the ranch house and you got it made and heck, I can't see anyone near that first stable as I squelch the urge to break into a heart-pounding run.

Yup, the last thirty yards were a mind's worth of miles.

Getting behind the stable, I left the fence line, slowed at the building's corner, and peered down the alley. I saw a long line of stalls with a half-dozen horses, heads out of their wooden nooks, one lazily shaking its mane.

Well, Ace, I thought, luck's got your kiss tonight.

The short ton of fear and nerve in my gut no longer weighed as much. I stepped around the corner.

A car was rolling to a stop at the far end of the second stable, its bumper and white hood just visible. I dropped the rake and vaulted over the gate of an empty stall, slipped through the stall's rear exit and got into the feed hall. Better move now instead of later, I thought, running hunched down and causing a couple of already skittish animals to whine and bang their stalls. Doors slammed. Whoop! Now what. I caught a rafter and lifted myself up into a half-filled loft, started to sneeze then fought it off.

"There you go, girl, there you go."

It sounded like Dickson. "Hey . . . here." The lights went on in the long stable.

"That new filly's down back." It was Dickson, followed by a couple of other pairs of feet.

They passed below me and I peeked down and through a crack in the loft. Briefly, in a fast glance, I saw a black-haired man in a white suit.

"Here?" another voice asked.

"Seems awfuly skittish," a Spanish-sounding voice observed.

"It's that racing blood, my friend."

There was a pause. "If you say so . . . my friend." There was another pause, then the Spanish voice continued. "We were coming over here to talk about, ah, horses, privately . . ."

Dickson cleared his throat. "Why don't you get on back to the car, Marshall."

"Yes sir."

"And thanks for everything you done for Bennet, yuh heah?"

"Yes sir."

"I won't forget it."

"It's real sad, Mr. Dickson."

"Lots of things are, Marshall."

"I'm sorry we had to lose Bennet to get that nosy cop."

"Yeah, but you done good. 'Fore you go, you know where Blaine's at?"

Marshall seemed to hesitate. "Uh, Blaine left with Mr. Harrison, didn't he?"

Dammit, I thought, there goes my shot at Rawlins.

I could see Dickson through the crack. He was nodding. "Yeah, I guess he did at that. He'll be back 'fore long. You wait in the Caddy."

I heard the cowboy walk away. Dickson turned, stepping out of my sight.

"So, as I was going to tell you, Freddy, things have started getting pretty *tight* on my end." There was a whine in Dickson's voice, a whine that, if one thought about it, was always in his voice but only showed its true edges when Dickson's talk turned to plead. "Now I damn well *know* we've planned it all out and gone over the entire thang, through it and through, all up and up like we agreed," Dickson continued. "And I done my part. I've

been talking with Harry-son and his bunch, I've talked to
Gonzales up in Austin and he's ready to lean on Washington, that's what he told me, all *I* have to do is give him the
word. So I went and paid him and Harrison, and we're all
just tighter than shitflies, just as tight as tight can be. But,
well, you know, I guess I've been thinking some. There
was that snooping Ramirez over at the Masterson place,
then his buddy come over and—"

"And your dumbass redneck fucking shot Ramirez,
right?" Carrizo interrupted. "You whining turd. Why do
things get so hot all the sudden? You *wonder* why. Dumb-
fuck cop killer."

"Hey, I knowed you killed—"

"Shut your shitmouth." There was a moment of sharp
silence. "Ramirez was a big dude with DEA, huh? And
your top man, oh yeah, top man, he being top man tells me
you don't rate brains, no, Blaine dumbshit shoots him.
Why? White boy Blaine hate spics, that it? Oh no, you
say, why he's tighter than dogshit on—"

"Well, he ain't got—"

"Shut your shitmouth, you hear me?"

Dickson was stung. "I don't like hearing you talk down
to me like that, Freddy."

"And me, I don't care what you like, Señor Shitmouth. I
got too many of your tickets for you to even breathe if I
tell you not to, understand? The thing about cats like you,
the thing about you dudes is that, once it gets a little tight,
your mind goes around the bend. No nerves, Charlie,
that's it on a nail. No goddamn nerves. Now let me explain
the world to you, slow like. Blaine drops a cop—"

"Because he was getting snoopy, goddammit."

"Okay," Carrizo said, "I buy that. He was snoopy.
Christ!" he shouted. "All cops are snoopy, even ones you
pay. You don't think I know Ramirez was a cop? I've
known that straitlaced asshole for years. Jesus. Harrison
tells me he was a cop, I know Ramirez is a cop so you

know Ramirez is a cop. That Masterson bitch is FBI, how's that sit on your head, huh?"

Carrizo stepped beneath my break in the slats. I saw a diamond pin on his white lapel. "Well," he continued, "don't look so shiteyed. She's a cop, a bull, a pig, huh? And so fucking what if she and Ramirez root around? Pigs root and mess and crap and you can *allow* for that in this business, I mean, allow bucks for it. You can't stop'em, but you can buy off time, man, I mean that, time for you to do your thing." He stepped out of my sight. "Then you, and, man, I hold you responsible for your dumbshit top boy, you got to go and, ah, wreck the timetable after *I've* bought all the fucking tickets? Man, you can mess one scene."

"What about Ramirez's friend?"

"That dumb jock?" Carrizo laughed.

Yeah, I thought, I was worth a laugh or two. So what about me?

"Man, that dude got run around like everybody's Christmas turkey, near as I can tell."

"He really wasn't a cop?"

"Cop? He was just a fucking road bum Ramirez hired to fix some fence while his buddy agents are back in S.A. pushing paperwork like good little pigs. They arrested that dude just to get him out of their hair."

Dickson snickered and laughed.

"Can that horseshit, Dickson. I can't stand the whining way you laugh, man."

Dickson stopped. "I can't even laugh?" He sounded angry and nervous.

"You can't even puke right as far as I'm concerned."

There was another zone of silence and I heard a couple of boots shuffle. "Don't like that at all," Dickson said, his voice tinning, rising in pitch, "not at all. You hear me?" he shouted, voice stiffening.

There was a long, low whistle from Carrizo. "So what are you gonna do, *bolio,* shoot me? Put that piece of Saturday plastic away, toad, and I'll forget you ever tried to do that."

There was a long pause and I could almost hear Dickson think, shiver, then sigh. "I wish to God I'd never gotten into this."

Carrizo laughed. "God? Don't wish nothing to God, man. You're just a greedy little white bastard and you know it. Oil wells and dice, they're both gambling. Bad shit to get into my friend, bad shit."

"And drugs ain't?"

"Hey, my friend, why don't *you* tell *me* all about it? You're in the drug business in a big way and have been and I got a nice packet in a deposit box in Chicago that tells everybody just how you've been in it. It gets opened if I die or, ah, disappear? So you be nice now and no more triggers."

Both men stepped beneath the split board. I saw Carrizo punch Dickson's chest with his index finger. "I spent ten years setting up the most fast-shit drug operation on the border, and no dumb punk like you's going to put me out of business. But, man, you've gone and come that close," he said, separating his thumb and index finger, "that close. And I don't like that. I don't like that at all. You got me all clear, no fuzz between the ears, Charlie? Now we got a haul and a half moving up tonight, you know that, right?" Dickson seemed to nod his head. "It's gonna go through this ranch, but it isn't gonna stay at this ranch, and I know you don't know that 'cause that's a change." Carrizo punched Dickson again. "Two vans, and I mean moving vans, are gonna pull in here tomorrow morning at five o'clock. That B-25's gonna set down at five past six. Those trucks'll be moving at six fifteen."

"They'll move the grass that fast?"

"Grass? Man, this load is *sweet* stuff, coke and Mexican brown. And don't act like you don't know what that is, huh? Play dumb, hey, I'm no goddamn jury. It's smack, horse, *heroin,* good buddy. Do you ten-four? And I don't want you near here or around here or anywhere because you'll just *fuck it up* like you've come damn near doing with everything else. So I want you to split, see, get in that white gold Cadillac and drive down to Laredo. Go to Boys Town, get laid, get nasty drunk on me, okay? Sure, you'll have a cop on your tail, but get him laid too, huh? That's part of the game."

"Okay, okay. Then what?"

"What do you mean, then what?"

"What about later?"

"You mean your IOUs."

"I mean," Dickson said, "I *mean* my share."

Carrizo laughed. "Your IOUs are torn, man."

"I got in this for cash, Freddy."

"Cash? How much do you want? $100,000? $200,000?"

"Hey, if I get slammed by the cops, they'll take my property away."

"Only if they can prove you paid for it with drug money, baby. Don't cry on my shoulder. You inherited it. Tell'em that. tell'em you got it from your fine upstanding daddy. Don't worry Dolf, my boy, we'll do business again, when the heat's less intense. Besides, they don't want you, you know, they want me, and they think I'm in Monterrey or maybe Venezuela, huh? Shit, you can just scream you didn't know what was going on. Gonzales and Harrison are in the bag, they'll sit on some judge and make him about so tall." Carrizo was out of sight again. Dickson followed him, saying something I didn't quite catch. "A quarter of a million? Why, my friend, you ask for peanuts," Carrizo said sarcastically. "Why don't you ask me for a pint of golden blood?"

"A quarter of a million," Dickson said nervously, "just as part of my next advance. Do we agree on it?"

"Why, my friend, we shake on it."

I took a chance and peered around the corner of a bale. Dickson was shaking Carrizo's right hand, Carrizo's back to me.

"Okay," Dickson said, sounding both pleased and resigned, "and what do you want me to do with Blaine?"

"Do with him? Why nothing. Ah, hah. I must tell you this before I forget." Carrizo laughed again.

"What's funny?" Dickson said, frowning.

"I almost forget a very big something. You see my friend, I look out for you." Carrizo slapped Dickson on the shoulder. "The police, all the police, little pigs, big pigs, DEA and FBI, they plan on raiding your house tomorrow morning about seven o'clock."

"They what?"

"Ah yes, I have it on good authority, very good. Make sure Blaine is here, eh? Tell him that he's good for a million dollars should anything happen and some of us end up in jail. He is the only one who really knows anything, isn't he?"

Dickson nodded and said yeah. " 'Specially now that Bennet's dead. You really guaranteeing him a million?"

Carrizo shook his head slowly, side to side, and turned away from Dickson. He ran his hand through his shining black hair as I got a look at his face. "Man, is your name Doof or is it Dolf? You really dumb man, really dumb. Those cops know Blaine killed Ramirez, yeah? You think they'll wan' to take him alive?"

Dickson grinned. "I get it . . . I get it," he repeated.

They started walkinig up the feed hall to the far door.

"How's Harrison and the rest of 'em get out of this?" Dickson asked quietly.

Carrizo laughed, his white polyester suit giving one last

shake, and he said something about Freddy Carrizo does the thinking and Dickson is just, well, I didn't get the rest of it too clear at all.

Marshall came back in a couple of minutes and turned off the stable light.

I lay back in the hay, chewing on a stale piece of straw, just thinking about people and things, people like Freddy Carrizo, like Elaine Masterson, yeah, even the ole Christmas turkey, himself. And I thought about numerous *things,* things like 250,000 individual dollars. My.

Heck—there was no recession in the drug business, was there?

# 13

I LAY BACK IN the hay for the better part of an hour, sayin' slow it down, take a rest—my body aware of its aches. So I dozed for five minutes, heck, I hadn't really slept for twenty-four hours, I'd had my face beat and my ass good and kicked, I'd cut a cowboy in half with a submachine gun and moved out five rugged miles and back, running most of it with a helicopter for a hat. Yeah, I deserved a nod or two.

The javelina shot through my mind. I couldn't shake that pig off, its squeal, a funny, greasy squeal of absolute terror, absolute loss. At least Sanchez had been quiet when he died. Greasy, yeah, that was it all right. I bit down on my piece of straw. Greasy, what a word. I bet ole Fast Freddy must have soaked his hair in Wild Root or shampooed with Havoline. Motor Oil Man. Damn him, calling me everybody's Christmas turkey. Me? Ho-bo turkey. Carrizo was probably right.

Yeah, you had to admire Fast Freddy's element of

snazz, all white suit, diamond brooch, white shoes? Did he have on a pair of white shoes? I couldn't remember. Well, he wasn't a stupid toad like Dickson, no sir, Fast Freddy had brains and a hyper-quick mouth, a tough man with the put-down.

So I guess I had been the Christmas turkey. But Christmas is a big sort of deal. Naw, a scrawny rock rooster's more like it, that's me, yeah, served on nobody's birthday. I bit down on my shortening piece of straw. My back ached, my head hurt—did my head ever hurt, with a sunburned inside pain.

I must have dozed for five minutes.

I dreamed I was hunting a skunk, outside of Ponca City? No—a family of skunks, cat-grinning skunks beside a church, inside an empty auto plant, a plant with welding sparks for light and comfort.

I woke up and rubbed my forehead.

I needed to forget this sorry business. Elaine Masterson. Didn't I know she was too fancy? Federal agent, a rich-bitch undercover cop. That sure showed me something. Yeah, that was a sight better than most rich kids, their daddies and mommies making them twenty-six-year-old junior partners or fashion photographers or getting them reporter jobs with *The Washington Post* or something. DEA or FBI. Did I C-A-R-E? I thought about her legs and, yeah, her nonexistent smile. Cripes, I was supposed to be over this grade school crush. Me get a hard-on for a female cop? I flung a handful of hay up in the air, and it separated into a short rain of chaff. Dammit all, I thought that I was through with even thinking about her.

My ribs hurt, my calves hurt, my etceteras hurt. And that pig, Christ, he was in a world of hurt no more, or was he? What would it be like, being an animal like that? Would it be any different? I mean, they only have to worry about sex during the rutting seasons, don't they?

But what was that bleeding pig like, where was it now, in some gully, still hurting, chewing on the bullet—Jesus, a belly wound can drip forever, can't it? Drip drip drip, endless, indigestion like?

I saw Madre cut Sanchez, and the cowboy in blue go down, cut in half by 9-millimeter automatic fire. My head hurt like Nam again. Naw—this Christmas turkey had too much heart, too much heart. And if he was gonna live, he was going to have to eat some of it.

Blaine. Did I really want to kill Blaine? Him and me, were we that far off? Could I be him, if I had a long streak of active mean?

I didn't think so, but the idea struck me. Top man? I laughed, sort of like Carrizo laughed, but quiet laughter 'cause I hadn't forgotten where I was. Well, the top man was being set up for a drop. I pointed my finger, cocked my thumb, and held the fingernail. The difference between me and Blaine was, I decided, the *big* difference, was that I didn't think I'd have gone along with Dickson, moving from cattle into killing, from running ranches into running dope, but I didn't really know, did I? Hadn't I gone along with the lumber company and their little FAA scam? Hadn't I gone along with the Pentagon? Go along get along, from grade school to the grave. I'd been one ugly Pole, one typical all-world dumbo, mouthing off maybe and cutting up, but like the rest of us poor suckers in the human race I'd been tagging along in whatever was chic and current and powerful. We gonna change things, brother. We gonna do things, brother. We gonna get you all charged up, bro, thinking what you're thinking is you, then we gonna send you out front. It's all a big s'periment, see, to find out if you bleed, while you're out front. We gonna manipulate your one and only life, brother boy. Good God. Dickson had been one of the manipulators, now he was in the squeeze. And what a hollow, miserable excuse of a guy. Paco and Dickson, now they were light years apart. Paco was a decent guy, yeah, an all right.

I released my thumbnail and fired an invisible bullet into the cosmos. Pow. I didn't like anything at all about this drug business either, except for the sums of money. Grass? Big deal, huh. Mafia? Bad news. But grass could be a big deal, like the time Everson got stoned on that Thai stuff and flipped his Huey over. He was the only dude that survived that crash. Nine GI's didn't. The major wrote their mothers and said those guys were killed in action. Bad. Evil. Heroin? No need to go into that, not with this kid. I'd seen smack in Nam and, yeah, in Lansing. The TV store next to the welding shop did a big transfer business, 'til the cops raided it and shut it down. Still I'd open up at six in the morning and find at least two junkies on the sidewalk and in the gutter, soaking up the inner bliss and tranquillity, gray spit oozing out the side of a mouth.

And my back hurt and my stomach growled and goddamn I'd forgotten all about that snake. Well good, maybe I wouldn't become some neurotic ninny and remember everything. I smiled. Hadn't I caught that egg-sucker and wasn't that rattler tough? God, it had frightened the hell out of me. And I guess I'd scared the hell out of it. A blind toss and it lands on Bennet's neck. Well, given time and circumstances, it'd probably have gone and bit ole Bennet anyway.

I got myself a new piece of straw and rubbed my forehead.

And dozed for maybe five short minutes.

# 14

AND WOKE WITH A start. One of the horses down the stable hall was banging in its stall. I needed to piss pretty bad—and the wind was up a bit, cool enough that I could feel it, even inside the loft. Wind could spook a horse, couldn't it? The fast air howled across the roof, slowed, then sped up to another howl. The wind could spook me, I thought.

The stable light was off, and nothing was moving but the wind and the horse. I still didn't want to take any chances. I put my straw hat on, moved quietly to the edge, and looked around. The horse in the far stall seemed to quiet down some. A piece of chain rattled—then silence. I eased over the edge, held myself for a moment, then dropped silently to the floor, landing on a convenient pile of hay and muck.

I unzipped and proceeded to let it rip against the bottom half of a stall's Dutch door.

"Hey, Blaine. That you?"

The urine came out with a gush.

"Blaine ... jest a sec huh. I'm tightening up ... uh ... this belly cinch."

A cowboy spooked that horse.

"Blaine?"

I let off a muffled "Huh," trying to sound like Rawlins. Maybe I succeeded. The cowboy stuck his head out of the stall and looked down the feed hall. I could only tell he wore a cowboy hat and I couldn't see his face. Good—he couldn't see mine.

"Oh. Takin' a whiz," he said. He pulled his head back in the stall.

Fooled him. Blaine and I were about the same size, but more than anything, I reasoned, him mistaking me for Rawlins meant old Blaine was back in this zone. Right. But now this goat-roper in the stall was the immediate problem, and all I had were my fists. Dammit, I'd left the pipe I'd picked up by the compressor somewhere in the hayloft. This situation wasn't a bit good.

I zipped up and looked at my watch. Four fourteen! My God. Well, five minutes of sleep adds up—I'd worry about the time later.

So I walked down the hall to the open stall.

The cowboy was bending over, muttering to himself, trying to fix a saddle catch. "Always something, ain't it." He glanced at me. "I know I'm late so you don't have to yell. You really think those poachers'll be coming up from the south?" He looked at me. I didn't think. He must have seen the toe of a combat boot, if he saw that much in the meager light of the Eveready flash he had tied to a thong on the saddle.

The horse barely whinnied when the cowboy fell. "Easy," I said to the filly. Yeah, the man had a buck knife on his belt and I got it and cut three lengths of rope off his lariat and tied him hard. Now for his mouth. There was nothing for his mouth. I found a horse blanket and cut a thirty-inch swath about two inches wide. God, that would taste awful. It even smelled bad.

It made a damn good gag.

The man had a thirty-thirty lever-action saddle gun and a .38-caliber police special—weird gun for a cowboy. I put the revolver in a pocket of my denim jacket, examined the rifle, then jammed it back in its saddle case. A gallon canteen hung next to the saddlebag. I had to have a quick swig. The drink was long and full and got even longer. Hey, this dude laced his water with an ounce or two of Jack Daniels. Now could I ever get into that, sometime, but not now. I smiled. Going after poachers? Jack Daniels as chaser for his canteen? This kid and I could have gotten along.

I tried on his hat—a little snug but a better fit than the straw one. And besides, it was black.

I walked the horse out of the stall and down the hall. As a rider I'm pretty damn bad but not completely inexperienced. Cousin Pete and I'd go out occasionally and run down rabbits on this farm outside Ponca City. But this quarter horse filly seemed pretty calm and slow, not that I was going to have to ride her that far. I figured she'd be my cover—I'd be just another night rider out on his horse, looking for Foreman Rawlins.

A Jeep pulled up by the stable exit. I tried to halt the filly, but she put her nose on through and neighed. The Jeep had its lights on dim.

A flashlight played on the horse's head.

"Randall?" It was Blaine in the Jeep. A couple of more men on horseback rode up. I fingered the .38, knowing they had the real firepower. "You go get in the oak grove behind the hangar and wait there for Sutter and Mason. I'll be back there in an hour or so." There was a loud break of squelch on a two-way radio. Blaine drove off with a quick shift of gears.

I looked after him. There were two other men in the Jeep, and the barrel of a light machine gun jutting out of the back. Three more men on horseback followed the vehicle.

The Jeep cut its dimmers off as it drove away. I breathed and noticed that the wind had slowed down some, even quieted.

Behind the hangar, the oak grove, Sutter and Mason, Blaine in one short hour. Now I'd have the drop, as long as Blaine got there before the other two. And if the boys showed first, I'd make sure I had the drop even then. I gave the filly a pat and led her out of the stable and around to the south side, walking back toward the fence.

I thought I remembered a gate near the back, and there was a gate, a double one. I opened it, the creak loud and long. Now why the hell had the wind gone and died just when I needed it. The filly walked through and I followed, holding the leather rein. We plodded side by side, across the stallion's field, heading toward the tail end of the oak grove. With the moon long past set, the stars shone like hard dots, dots that already had a notion of their fate, the farthest eastern edge of the earliest twilight nudging against night's rim.

The filly stopped and took a bite of grass. I let her. We moved on as I looked at my watch. Four thirty-five. The plane comes in at six or so. Now, I thought, I'd like to watch that show, the bomber buzzing the top off that outhouse and avoiding those stumps. Maybe, just maybe there was enough room out there, but I wouldn't try it.

Short of the grove the filly took another nibble at the grass, whinnied, then raised her head. Well, she smelled the stallion's smell, okay girl, that's all right. I gave her rein a tug.

She bolted as the butt end of the rifle missed me and

slammed into her neck. I drove my knee up into the man, a man in black, swinging my two fists like a mace at where I thought his head should be.

There was an oof of escaping air and I whirled and dove into the oak grove as a different black body intercepted mine with a thigh-pinning tackle. I landed on a root and lost my breath.

Someone jammed a silencer against my jaw.

"You breathe and you die."

"F—FFF—Fernando!?" I wheezed it out.

"Buchanan," he said. He had black cork under his eyes and wore a black stocking cap over his ears. He pushed my head flat into a pile of oak leaves and fell flat beside me, the gun only momentarily parting from my temple. "Talk quiet," he whispered sharply.

"Uh," I managed, feeling around for my cowboy hat. It wasn't there. I wasn't thinking too straight either.

"Hands and knees, crawl low and fast. Back there. Even think of shouting and you're a dead man." He pushed me with the pistol and I started crawling back down the grove. To my left I saw one, two prone people, both of them cradling M-16's. Yeah—federal firepower by Mattel.

Fernando stopped me beside a tree and signaled with his hand. "Move back five feet." I did, crawling on my belly.

Elaine lay beside another man with cork blacking his eyes and a knit cap on his head. He grinned at me. I recognized the man from the beige Ford. Fernando pushed me flat again and said something just above the inaudible. The man from the beige Ford nodded and rolled away.

Elaine had a radio set on her back, the fancy air force FAC type with an earphone and a pilot's head mike. She signaled to Fernando, meaning for him to wait.

"It's Buchanan," Fernando whispered.

"Thought so," she said, tapping what looked to be a

cigar-size starlight scope. "How come he isn't tied and gagged?"

Oh no, I thought.

"He almost broke Jose's chest, Masterson," Fernando said angrily. Fernando put his silenced pistol to my head. "What's your story?"

"I'm ... I," I fumbled.

"Calm down," Elaine whispered slowly.

"I come over here to ..." I thought a moment, totaling things up, "to kill Blaine Rawlins."

Elaine seemed to smile. I didn't look at Fernando's face. The starlight, pale, made ever paler by the trees and dawn, still caught her face—except where she hadn't put on black cork to damp down the reflection.

"Well, did you kill him, Bill?"

I shook my head and said no, not yet. "But I will soon—real soon."

Fernando said he was going back up to Jose and the others. "Unless you still want me to tie him up." He lingered a moment.

"Forget it," Elaine said. Fernando crawled off. "So what have you been up to?" she asked me.

I started to tell her, beginning somewhere in the middle, I thought, no, with sneaking off from the bunkhouse, that's where I started.

"Shhh." She raised her hand. She spoke into the head mike. "Roger, Echo Echo. That's our grid ... you got it right?"

Heck, I knew this jargon by heart.

"Out," she said. "Now, after you stole my truck."

"I didn't steal your truck. It's down by the ridgeline in the mesquite brush. I left the key in the ignition." She seemed to nod.

"Okay," she said blankly.

I paused. "Something the matter?" I asked.

She shook her head. "Too much hiss in this receiver."

She tapped the headphones with her fingernail. I picked up the economy-size Starlight scope and flipped what looked like the switch. It came on and I pointed it across the field. There was almost too much early morning twilight. I could see the ranch houses, a blotch of light where the windows were. I saw my filly with my carbine walking back toward the grove.

Elaine took the scope from my hand and shut it off. "Keep your butt down," she told me.

I lay there another long ten or twelve minutes.

"Right," she said into the mike. "You got it right ... affirmative." She sounded tough and hard and involved.

"You all waiting for the six o'clock flight?" I asked her. "Or is this the seven o'clock raid I've fallen in with?"

She looked at me and blinked. "What are you talking about?"

I told her I'd overheard Dickson and Freddy Carrizo. "You what?"

I told her all about the seven o'clock raid by big and little pigs. "And the six o'clock arrival. But that's the moving vans to Chicago. The plane with the Mexican smack gets here at five after six."

"You *saw* Freddy Carrizo here?" she asked incredulously.

"Yeah," I said, looking at my watch. It was almost five fifteen. Blaine oughtta be coming back. Well, Fernando would kill him with that silenced pistol, and I'd have to be satisfied with that, a soft pffft and Rawlins toppling to the dirt. I didn't like killing anyway, I kept seeing the blue cowboy caving in half. The pig, too. Heck, from a chopper I'd seen men fall, but then I was gone, away at ninety knots or more. I never stayed to view my own results, though I'd seen the work of others, stuff too ugly, so real it was unreal. GI body bags after the Michelin. The dumdum wound in what was Paco's back. No end to it.

Another five minutes or so passed. Elaine was jamming

a button on her radio. She reached around her back and tried to slam the bottom of the radio carrier. "See if that battery's in straight," she ordered. I did. Her bottom was on straight, too.

"It's fine," I said.

I saw her eyes and they were lovely and I felt sort of afraid of her—and sort of lonely. Since I'd hung around this long I had to find out what lay at the end of the rainbow.

So I leaned over to kiss her, nice and wet.

She met my lips with a set of muddy fingers. "I don't deal in impulse," she said coldly.

I guess not.

"You really saw Carrizo here? What did he say?" I started to tell her. "Speak up," she said.

"He and Dickson yell at each other like a couple of mad dogs. Carrizo's one tough dude."

"*What* did he say? the plane's coming at six?"

"Yeah." I looked at her, still wanting to kiss her. "Five past six."

"It's arriving at seven," she said flatly.

"Huh?"

"It's supposed to fly in here at seven with a load of grass."

"That's not what I heard them say."

"Our *intelligence* says seven." She clicked the radio band controls. "Shit," she hissed, "this thing has to be working, so answer me, will you!" She looked up for a moment, at the canopy of oak leaves in the dawn light. I heard the call of a distant dove.

"Who you trying to reach? Those barns may be interfering with the line of sound, iffn you're trying to reach somebody on the other side."

"I'm trying to reach a helicopter."

And my mind clicked on. "A chopper."

"Yeah, do you mind?"

"A chopper as a radio link?"

She didn't answer, she ignored me. "Go get Fernando. He's got another radio up there. Tell him I can't reach Harrison."

"Harrison—as in lieutenant colonel, deputy commander of the DPS?"

"Yes."

"Carrizo and Dickson were talking about him. I saw a state chopper land here yesterday morning and Blaine said Harrison was in it."

Elaine looked at me intently. "Harrison's working as a double."

"Gee," I replied.

She paused. "But you say he's been in touch with Carrizo?"

"According to what Carrizo said."

Elaine cursed.

"What's s'matter. I ain't lying."

She stared hard at the ground. "I changed our plan this morning when we jumped two cowboys southwest of here. All the other tactical teams are at least a kilometer back. I got us in closer."

She sounded like she was talking to herself.

"So," I said.

"The last thing I told Harrison was where we'd moved to. He said that was shit, but to stay put and he'd get back to me."

"So?"

"So goddammit. A little over an hour ago six guys in a Jeep with a radio and a light machine gun go off to the south, toward where we're supposed to be, like they're off to get in a gun fight. Like they knew we were coming, huh?" I just listened to her. "You think that doesn't set me to thinking something's going wrong? Then I tell Harrison we're here and he sounds double-pissed." She tapped the Starlight scope. "Damn," she said softly.

"That was Blaine in the Jeep," I said. "Hey—the cowboy I hit, 'fore I hit him, said something about going after poachers to the south."

Elaine rolled onto her side. "Harrison was to work with Dickson. He's never said anything about talking to Carrizo." She paused. "Freddy is very big game."

"So Harrison should have said something to you, huh?" I asked lazily.

"Dammit. I'm scrubbing this mission," she said, starting to crawl off.

I grabbed her by the pants pocket. "What about the plane?"

"Let it land and fly off. I don't want dope, I want dope dealers—and maybe a fucked-up cop. You stay put. You're now state's evidence." She started to crawl away.

The grenade went off just before the flare. I saw a body bounce from exploding earth and rise in a fast-slow flip. Blindness from flarelight and a light machine gun opened up with lead hail.

I rolled on top of an M-16, then the dead body of the man from the beige Ford. In a swoop I had the M-16 on full auto and I sprayed low along the fence line, guessing, then spotting the rattling red bark of the mg's paced fire. I kept rolling until I slammed against an oak. The flare had sputtered. Fernando stood momentarily framed, the combination rifle-and-grenade launcher at his shoulder. He fired toward the barns, then broke at mid-belly as a carbine spit and pumped a second round into his collapsing body.

I couldn't see Elaine. I switched to semiauto to save ammo and looked. I heard a couple of groans in front of me, and then three small caliber shots jumped off the top of the far barn. One of the bodies beneath the trees screamed a man's scream as I put two rounds of return fire just above the gable on the barn roof. You could see the body roll hard down the metal roof and fly off the ledge like a loose jointed sack.

I crawled up the slope toward the wounded.

Elaine tapped me on the thigh—it had to be her touch. "Good shot. Now listen, Buchanan. I've got to get out of here."

"You've got to get out of here!" A pistol round smacked into the oak behind us. "What about my ass? I ain't a cop."

She unhitched the radio rig from her back. "This was a fucking setup. Five agents are dead and the rest of a multimillion-dollar investigation's in here." She pointed to her head.

A couple of more rounds, rifle rounds, slammed into a tree. Someone was working his way around our flank.

My eyes had gotten over the flare and in the coming dawn light I could see where Blaine's boys had put their machine gun. What a stupid place, right under the rail. Those cowboys weren't ready to fight any drug war. I must have nailed two of 'em with one burst.

"Are you listening to me?" she demanded.

I looked at Elaine. What a bitch. Man, the two of us pushed to the ground by gunfire, her buddies shot to scabs, and she's thinking about dollars and police budgets and her own private ass. "What the hell am I supposed to do, lady? Rear-guard it?"

She leaned over and kissed me hard and quick, not a kiss of want or a kiss of need but a dirty kiss of I-demand-something and something-awful-damn-soon.

"Why not?" she said.

Lord—I was a pair of lips attached to a momentary hero.

"Are 'Nando and Jose dead?"

172 · AUSTIN BAY

I think she nodded yes. She picked up a submachine gun, made sure it was cocked, then looked at me. "You got another magazine of M-16 rounds?"

"No."

"Now you do," she said, handing me one. "You spray it down as I go. I'm going to run back down the grove and get the hell out of here."

"You cover me when I follow you?"

"Sure," she said quickly.

Another pistol round kicked up dirt. I opened up in the gunfire's general direction and Elaine took off, spraying the front and then the side toward the fence.

A rifle opened up behind me. I turned and caught two men about thirty yards away. Elaine was down the grove, going hard, two elbows and one asshole, so to speak. I kept shooting. No one was shooting back. Then I was out of ammo.

I looked up. A man, a man without a rifle, was running down the fence line. It was Blaine.

I took a chance and stood up, then ran toward the end of the grove, almost tripping on Fernando's body.

No one fired at me. I glanced over my shoulder. Elaine was nowhere in sight. Nothing. I tossed my empty rifle away. It bounced against a tree. Blaine paused. In the red morning light his eyes looked like burnt red glass. From beside Fernando's body I picked up another M-16.

Blaine was running down the wide alley between the two barns.

I broke toward the fence line. "Blaine," I yelled. "Stop or you're dead." He glanced over his shoulder. I pulled the trigger. Nothing happened. The rifle was out of ammo.

Blaine fired a pistol shot that put brass tacks in my ear. That was heavy lead—.45-caliber. I dropped the rifle, pulled the .38 out of my jacket and fired back. He ducked into the hangar barn's first side door as I slid under the fence and ran to the hangar's side. Pressing flat against the metal wall, I moved to the door, waiting for the slightest motion. I didn't like this position at all, so I dove past the door and fired. There was a returned shot, from deep inside the hangar, a shot that hit just inside the door frame, smacked something hard, and gave off with a whine.

There was a second side entrance to the barn, up toward the front. I ran down the alley, checked my rear, lay down and inched around the door corner. Good, a bale of hay.

Someone had opened the main hangar door. I could see the rising light in the east—and the King Air as gone, parked about two hundred yards away, out by the stump field. Well, with the door open that was one less wall to have to worry about covering, and it did shed some light on where Blaine was hiding.

Brrrang!

Blaine put a high round into the metal wall, knocking loose some chains. He was guessing, the fool. I couldn't tell just where the shot came from, but it seemed he was shooting at a diagonal to me—say, across the building and near the back?

A machine, the air compressor, began to cough, then run at a low hum. The three air lines, instead of inflating, collapsed.

I checked my .38. Four shots, and they'd all have to count. Well, let's make some count more than others.

I could see the barrel of aviation gas on the metal dolly. Was it still full? I squeezed off a shot and the round whacked the barrel's side. The increasing sunlight revealed a stream of gas falling on the dirt below.

"Shaakk!" Blaine was yelling something.

"Blaine," I called, pressing down against the hay bale. "It's me. Buchanan."

"I knew you were a cop," he replied, shouting.

"You're wrong Blaine."

Whap—another .45-round pounded into the loft above the door.

I took another shot at the av gas and either missed it or it just didn't go.

"If you ain't a cop, then why are you shooting at me?" he said, almost asking, with a slow cadence.

The av gas still dripped from the suspended drum.

"You killed a friend of mine, Blaine."

"I kicked your ass," he yelled, ripping off two rounds, and moving up from behind the av gas can and firing one more sparking round from his automatic pistol, he fell toward cover behind a bale just as the pistol's spark caught vapor, rich gasoline vapor, and with a short breath ignited in an orange ball and blossom that seemed to bounce Blaine against the hay bale, pick him up and toss him like a fiery, burning rag toward the hangar door.

I slammed against the hay bale as the heat surge blew past me, then I pushed back out the side door, scrambling away, toward the field, trying to escape the next explosion. My God. More gasoline. Flame and black smoke belched through the yawning hangar door.

I ran. Now where?

Nowhere, I thought, feeling naked, a target, perfectly exposed. There was the King Air and that ill-shaped outhouse-like building. I had two .38 rounds left. Not enough. Somebody might be in the plane—I'd better take the building. I ran maybe fifty yards and stopped in my tracks. The building and, yeah, at least a dozen of the large tree stumps were wavering, collapsing—dammit, *deflating,* rubber without air. "Hah!" came on like an orange light in my brain and I turned boots and nose toward the aircraft.

It was close to five-fifty and the bomber hadn't come yet. Well, that slow mail might get here late, but Bill Buchanan was gonna hop the unexpected express plane out. If he could get it started.

The cabin entrance was unlocked and open. I jumped in, landing on one of the plush executive seats. Nobody was inside.

Huh—air-filled obstacles. Jesus, what a stretch of the pocketbook. Who'd these guys plan on fooling, besides me? I mean, hadn't that stuff looked plenty real enough to me? Rubber rooms for the blind. A buried hose and an electric plug, well, maybe. Jesus in camouflage. And it fooled all hell out of my calibrated eyes.

I moved to the controls. Yeah, I could fly this crate. I'd flown light planes and that's like bicycling—once you learn, you don't forget. Helicopters, now that was real flying, like balancing on a bucking egg. This Beech would be a dream.

I saw the plane, it wasn't a B-25, but a DC-3, painted black, engines loud as a dozen piston-driven hives. It came racing down the horizon and landed, its wheels touching at the very tip of the deflated building, just beyond a blinking red light that flipped out, then immediately shut off. The bomber kicked up dust and landed hard, went into a controlled skid and whipped a turn to the right, stopping on something just short of a half dollar. Not bad—no, damn good. Helluva pilot.

I could see two trucks rolling off the road, coming to meet the plane, big trucks, the vans no doubt. Well, the plane might have been a bit early, but all in all this was pretty well timed, a criminal ballet, with a large white car, a convertible, a white Cadillac convertible leaving the vans, spinning out, then heading toward the King Air. I started to flip one of the ignition switches, then stopped. This was a ballet, all right. A helicopter, yeah, the state police Jet Ranger, Colonel Harrison's I presume, was shooting across the landing field about six feet off the turf, running lights on, swirling police color like a high-speed pinball machine.

The Caddy's lights flicked on and off.

No shit—Freddy Carrizo was riding shotgun in the Caddy, a tall, thin Anglo at the wheel. The chopper hovered and began to land. The Cadillac stopped about fifty feet from the King Air, and Carrizo pulled a pistol from his coat and shot the driver through the head—right through the head, like someone shoots a broke-leg horse.

"C'mon!" Carrizo was yelling at the two troopers. He had two bags in his hand and he ran toward the King Air. The two troopers bailed out of their helicopter and followed him, both hatless, both with silvered sunglasses, their gray uniforms and block boots pounding across the field.

Damn. And I had two rounds. Well, I always wanted to hijack a plane to Cuba. Maybe we'd take this one to Miami. I slipped into the King Air's tiny lavatory, squeezing against the john seat and closing the thin plastic door.

Carrizo climbed aboard, followed by another, hard breathing voice. "Goddammit, Freddy," the voice was saying.

"No! No!" Carrizo shouted. "This plane and now. Argue later."

I heard the other trooper climb aboard.

"Wind this thing, Mitch," the first trooper's voice ordered.

"You bet, Colonel."

So, as I'd thought, enter the colonel himself.

Well, Elaine had run off. And ole dumb bunny me, I was gonna wrap up a big state cop and serve him on a platter. Would that impress that bitch? God, she was strange.

Carrizo cursed out a line of hot Spanish and then the engines fired, number one and number two.

"Hot damn. Five million bucks!" Harrison yelled.

"It better be," Carrizo sounded nasty.

"You didn't check?" the colonel asked in disbelief.

"Chicago wouldn't cross me," Carrizo said sourly, his voice rising as the engine revs reached a higher pitch.

"Well, fuck me but it looks like it's all real," Harrison said. He had opened one of the briefcases.

The plane pitched forward as we taxied. "Get ready." It was the pilot, Mitch whatever. "We're going up fast."

The engines jumped down my ears and I fell back against the lavatory wall as the plane accelerated, bumped on the rough field, bounced, ran, ran, and bounced off again, falling, then staying aloft.

Carrizo shouted something.

"Tell 'im to keep this sucker low," Harrison yelled. "There's gonna be a hornet's nest of planes up damn quick."

Harrison had to be right outside the lavatory door.

The plane roared on for about a minute and a half.

"Hey, Mitch?"

I thought I heard a yelled "yes sir" over the engine noise.

"Keep this thing level for a minute, y'heah? I gotta piss."

Oh no. I cocked the pistol.

Harrison opened the door and I put a round in his big chest, his right arm flying up to grab me as I fell. The plane jolted, swerved, Harrison going back against the cabin exit, his gray head cracking against the plane's low roof.

Carrizo didn't waste time trying to bullshit. He had a tiny ladies' automatic, maybe .25-caliber, and his arm was swinging, as if in slow motion, bringing the weapon toward my side. Then the plane jerked again, just as I fired at Fast Freddy. Fwomm. The plane bucked up, pitching

Carrizo back toward me, pressing me against Harrison's body as the aircraft barrel-rolled right, then straightened and barrel-rolled left.

"I'm hit!" the pilot screamed. "My God, I'm hit!"

Carrizo, gunless, scrambled back into the middle of the craft, hanging on to a seat. I threw my empty pistol and missed. Carrizo reached to his lapel and grasped the big diamond brooch, whipping it across his face with a flash.

It was a razor.

He sneered a sneer that began just below his nose and ran out to the ends of his long black mustache, and he began cutting back and forth with his razor, slicing out an imaginary belly in the air.

"Who're you!" he shouted, voice quavering. Tough, hard, yet scared—his eyes had the look of the frightened rattler.

I didn't say anything. I grinned.

Carrizo broke the air with his diamond edge. *"Who are you?* Don't you understand English? Habla español?"

I must have laughed. "Si. Comprendo."

Carrizo lashed with the razor, missed me, and cut off a shear from the top of one of the overstuffed executive seats.

"You want cash, cowboy? Eh, cabrón? Cash? How much?"

I thought a second. He was offering me money.

"Cash? I'll give you a bundle."

I stopped for a second. "Hey—"

Carrizo lunged with the diamond-studded razor, the slash ripping part of my denim jacket, and the airplane tipped violently to the right, throwing him against the windows, his arm catching the corner of the lavatory door, cracking, and going up at a radical angle.

I kicked out, missed his head with my boot, but fell back, driving my elbow into the back of his neck.

He collapsed.

The pilot was moaning, not softly. Hell, he was shouting.

I clambered over Carrizo's body and got to the pilot. "Better hurry, man," he muttered, "if you want to come down in one piece. I'm feeling a little . . . little cold."

I looked at the wound in his right shoulder. "Hang on," I said. "You'll make it." I grabbed the first aid kit from beneath the copilot's seat and tore it open, getting an emergency tourniquet. With the scissors I cut off Mitch's blood-soaked shirt and applied the bandage, wrapping it over his shoulder and under his arm. "With some luck and a little chewing gum you're gonna get through this," I told him.

He gave a weak grin. "It's pretty bad, isn't it?"

"I don't think so. I've seen a lot worse."

It was bad. The worse ones I'd seen had always died.

I slid into the copilot's seat and took the twin control. "Where're we headed?" I asked.

Mitch looked at me for a moment. "Can you fly?"

I nodded. "You wanta go for a hospital in San Antone?"

Mitch sighed. "No. Mexico," he said softly, "this grid." He pointed to a plastic-covered map. "F—" he paused and winced, "Freddy's folks are supposed to meet us there."

I took the controls. We were a couple of hundred feet off the deck and we were heading due east. I kicked us up to five hundred feet and went into a bank, bringing us back to a west-southwest course.

I kept my eyes straight ahead and brought us back to the deck, below air control, about one hundred feet above the dry landscape. "I don't really like the idea of Freddy's people," I said.

I glanced at Mitch. He stared at me, a funny look in his bloodshot eyes. "I bet . . . you got a dead Fred in . . . the back. Don't you?"

"Might have to stop to dump some trash, huh?" I smiled.

I checked my altimeter and brought the plane up a little. "I think you're better off going to San Antone, my friend."

Mitch put a pistol to my head.

He locked his teeth in a hard clench. "Freddy's people won't believe shit about Freddy." He breathed heavily. "They'll know one of us killed him . . . and after all . . . you wrecked him, huh?"

I looked at Mitch. He had more grit than I'd thought, and more energy. I swallowed the heart that had found a home in my throat. That pistol barrel felt like a cold arrow from hell, just waiting, sitting against my temple, suspended from its inevitable release.

"C'mon, Mitch . . . reason with me for a second. You don't want to go to jail, right? Bet you don't want to bleed to death either. Is it the money . . . hell, then let's fly this thing to . . . Sanderson," I said, locating a name on the map.

He shook his head. "No dice, cowboy . . . they've got my wife down there as security, so you see," he said, poking my head with the automatic, "I don't have any choice . . . too bad you killed Freddy. But I'm feeling a little stronger as . . . it is. Maybe I shouldn't even try and keep you al—"

I jammed the control down and brought my arm up underneath the gun. Mitch screamed in pain and I caught the King Air about forty feet off the deck, straightened it out with one hand, the other fist slamming into his wound.

I got the pistol and hit him across the face. He slumped forward, moaning.

I tried to see my reflection in the cockpit window. There was nothing there. Mitch gave a cold moan. He looked very worn and pale.

I've gotta get out of this bitch, I screamed. I know I must have screamed from blood, giving the King Air every horse its engines had. Somewhere, sometime, out, just away, out of the bitch I'd fallen into like a one-way seed thrown nowhere.

Cattle, Brahman and shorthorn ran like mice from the low shadow of the plane, then I skimmed cacti, short scrub, a few miserable live oak about a watering hole, and on, due west, revved at 210 miles an hour.

Two dead men, one dying, and a looney tune, me, the almost looney, tearing up the air at 210 per.

I rubbed my two-day growth of beard. It itched. Yeah, I was still here, wasn't I? Jesus, deflating stumps and rubber buildings, stone-cold female cops, two fresh bodies, soon to be a third, and a score of other stupid, violent men, men a lot like me.

And five million bucks in a couple of briefcases.

I hadn't really thought about that.

Saliva ran from Mitch's mouth. He slumped farther down in his seat.

I bounced the plane up for five hundred feet. Way to the north I could see a small town, northeast now. I bounced back down. What, fifteen miles? I looked at the map. Where the hell was I? Who the hell knew where I was and who I was and who the hell but me cared?

Did I care?

I decided I didn't. As long as five million bucks was behind me.

Due west, now running at a southwest-to-northeast diagonal, was a long two-lane hardball. I followed it for a couple of minutes, then saw on the horizon its intersection with another two-lane highway.

I flew over the intersection.

Had I seen a car? I jumped up to a thousand feet and circled, banking to the south. Nothing coming up the north-south hardball from that direction. I got back to eight hundred and ran north for a couple of minutes. No cars or houses that I could see, at least for ten clear miles or so.

Well, thank the Lord for the room in Texas, where engineers can make highways like they dream them, long and straight, uncurved. Gauging the fences and the telephone pole just to the left shoulder of the road, I started my landing, north to south.

It was a piece of cake. I taxied a couple hundred yards, then shut the plane down, turning it so that the aircraft blocked the highway.

Mitch was out completely. I felt his neck—it grew colder. Popping open the first briefcase, a black aluminum Zero-Halliburton job, I counted twenty bundles, each bundle with ten stacks of a hundred-dollar bills in little paper wrappers. Figure a hundred hundreds to each wrapper. What a heist. Two million. I shut the briefcase.

Yeah, I wasn't greedy.

I looked at Mitch. Mitch couldn't even manage a moan.

There was a weedy looking green-flowered carpetbag lying on one of the seats. I unzipped it and tossed out its contents, a can of beer falling on the seat as well as some clothes. A few things stuck in the bag. I let'em stay. I slid the aluminum briefcase into the carpetbag and threw the beer can back in for good luck, zipping the bag tight.

I went to the rear of the cabin and opened the exit door, tossing the carpetbag to the ground.

Naw. I wouldn't be stupid for a change. For a change, yeah, Billy Buchanan was going to get to really finish a job.

I saw Carrizo's diamond razor lying on the floor and I put it in my jacket pocket. "C'mon, Mitch," I said, grabbing his limp body. His .32-caliber pistol still sat on my pilot's seat. I slipped it in the jacket pocket with the razor and dragged Mitch to the cabin door, then I went back to the front seat and found the second briefcase.

Mitch's aviator gloves, a fabric military pair, lay on the floor. Good idea. I put them on. I opened the second brief-case—thirty stacks, three million bucks. I closed the case and picked up from the back of a seat a dirty white shirt I'd tossed out of the carpetbag. Inside Corrizo's white coat pocket I found a cheap butane cigarette lighter.

Okay, I thought, all set. I threw everything I needed out the door onto the asphalt.

"Your turn, Mitch ole buddy."

I pulled Mitch out of the plane, carefully, making sure his wound spilled just a little, a few red droplets here, more there, as I lead him, carried him down the highway, stopping only once, about fifty feet away, to plant *his* foot firmly in one of the spills, then bringing him toward the shoulder of the road, maybe seventy feet from the air craft. There. I let him fall. He bled a little more and didn't move.

I ran back to the aircraft, stood about twenty feet away, careful not to muss Mitch's red brown trail, and fired two rounds of .32-caliber into the underside of the wing, just below the fuel tank.

She didn't explode, thank goodness. I sighed in relief. A small but steady stream of aviation fuel poured onto the highway. I picked up the dirty white shirt, sopped it in the gas, then climbed up beside the fuel tank cowl and popped it open. I stuffed the half-soaked shirt into the fuel intake and slipped off the wing, moving back to my carpetbag.

I looked at the pistol then threw it back inside the airplane door.

Carrizo's lighter hit on the first flick. I stuck the flame on the shirt's dry cuff and held it there until it took, then grabbed my green-flowered carpetbag with the two million and the briefcase with the three million and raced up the highway.

It still hadn't gone when I reached Mitch. I dropped the briefcase with the three million so that it fell against his knee and toppled onto his hand, then I moved his fingers so that two of them hooked the handle, natural like.

Now blow, you rotten piece of metal.

The shirt was a complete blaze and the fuel on the asphalt had caught a shallow flare, but the plane wasn't exploding. Well, I wasn't gonna wait. Let'em find my fingerprints inside—these boots were moving.

I ran up the road and the airplane blew up in a high orange, then black fireball, becoming thick hydrocarbon smoke.

I ran, north, the full sunrise to my right, thinking about nothing, thinking about two million bucks, about my step after next step, about Elaine.

Elaine.

To hell with Elaine.

And her forty-dollar check—that'd be one check I'd never cash. By damn, there'd be other women. I thought of Anne. Lonely, easy Anne—lonely. She'd liked me when I was low. Well, hadn't she, in her own pale way?

I ran for about six or seven minutes, really ran, then looked back once again, licking the salt sweat off my lips. The blaze roared on. Another two minutes of roadwork and I stopped, breathing hard. I must be better than a mile north of that blaze by now.

And I saw what I was looking for.

Across the fence line, not more than a half mile away as the crow flies, in the midst of the desert, was a stand of oak, their peaks capped by a windmill blade. I walked to the road's shoulder, leaped over the gravel and well into the grass, and picked my way through the six-foot barbed wire fence.

A windmill, yes, I'd risk it there, I'd wait it out. I took an easy lope across that last half mile, taking another ten minutes to cover it, making sure I didn't leave any tracks to this place off the road, alone—and I collapsed against a thin oak, my fall shaking loose a shower of dried leaves.

I breathed hard for a couple of minutes and looked at my watch. Whew. I went a little farther into the grove.

Ten or eleven minutes later I heard a siren, a distant pulse of low-frequency electric thunder, now drowned by the thrummm of aircraft engines.

I slipped a little deeper into the trees and green.

It was an air force spotter plane, OV-10. It circled the fire a couple of times and shot south down the road, then came back just north of the wreck and dropped a little red magnesium warning flare.

Silly-ass Air Force. The red flare sputtered and died. Well, the King Air was likewise pretty well reduced to slag.

The spotter plane did one last wheel and then headed north and east toward San Antonio, I suspected, and the sounds of the car sirens came closer.

I watched them wander around the wreck, there in that distance, for more than an hour. More and more cars, police, sheriffs, deputies, firemen, newsmen, gawkers, and, yeah, three or four looping buzzards, buzzards to be disappointed by the coroner, buzzards who would later swoop down to that dark, burned spot and pick their beaks among the hard metal ruins.

A couple of patrol cars drove slowly along the highway then back, and nothing came of their trips. I laughed and drank the warm Miller beer in my carpetbag, crushing the golden can after I'd finished the liquid. There was an apple in the bottom of the bag, partially smashed by the briefcase but still edible. I munched it, then tossed the core and the empty beer can back in the carpetbag—I'm no Johnny Appleseed, but I'm not a litterer either.

Christ in heaven, yeah Lord, I felt good. Damn good.

The sun was up and what clouds had lingered with this morning were long torn away. The day would be a blazer, yes sir, a damn fine blazer. I shooed a yearling calf out of my way and walked to the windmill. No, I wouldn't be stupid and untether the pump. Some sharp-eyed county deputy would spot those spinning, working blades, and he'd come and investigate before I'd have a chance to split.

Sunlight reflected off the mill blades.

I looked down into the limpid brickstone reservoir, the water surface rippleless, unblemished. Whoop! Didn't like what I saw. Two bagged eyes and an age of angry dirt. I splashed some water in my face and took a long, cool drink of the sweet liquid.

Well, I still had a wait on my hands.

Then I looked down at my reflection, this time rolling, enlarging, and contracting in the waves.

Yes, something could be done.

Hey, Billy Buchanan, I said out loud, to the cows, to the water, to the world that mattered, you look like you're on the bad side of scraggly, son, and you weren't raised to look like trash. No doubt about it, man—you sure as hell can use a shave.

Pulling out the diamond razor, I grabbed hold of the carpetbag's leather handle and started using it for a strop.